STORIED CROSSINGS

Anthology of Award-winning Short Stories

ISBN-13: 978-0-9742652-0-9
ISBN-10: 0-9742652-0-9

DEDICATION

This anthology is dedicated to those who live to imagine

To the authors featured in this book: Scribes Valley thanks you for your time, patience, trust, and talent.

TABLE OF CONTENTS

WRITING THE PERFECT STORY
A Foreword by David L. Repsher, editor

THE PERFECT STORY. Now there's something you'll probably never see. It ranks right up there with the Loch Ness monster, the Abominable Snowman, and a politician with a conscience. But that doesn't stop us writers from trying to create one. Every time we sit in front of a word processor, our heads bursting with ideas that will get us worldwide recognition, something happens and the ideas die almost before they're born. It's a struggle, plain and simple. The cause of sleepless nights and countless headaches. Still we trudge on toward the battle. Why? Let's see if I can elucidate that point a little for you.

First off, my name is David and I'm a human. Okay, I know that's a weird way to introduce myself, but it's necessary. You see, I'm saddled with an imagination the size of the Third Quadrant of the Gamma Sector in the Plutonious System located at the butt-end of the known Universe. And I share this imagination with someone else: David the writer. Although we're as separate and distinct as peanut butter and jelly, we are still one entity, trying to co-exist in a happy, creative environment where the ideas and words flow like suntan oil on a Swedish supermodel. And that actually happens.

About twenty percent of the time.

Now, as we set in front of the word processor, I have decided that once again we will undertake the colossal task of writing the perfect story. You, our readers, are invited along for the ride. Please stay seated and keep your hands and feet inside because we never know just where this process will take us. Here we go.

It's about time! You really do ramble a lot.

Sorry about that. Are you ready?

You bet. What's the subject this time?

I don't know.

Wow, we're off like a herd of turtles.

Hey, just slapping words on paper has started some of the greatest stories ever written. Why don't you throw something out and we'll build on it?

It was a dark and stormy night. The bridge was gone, washed away in the raging torrent that used to be Oceanstreamriver creek. Trees were down everywhere and hundreds of puppies and kittens met their maker as the storm...

Stop.

What's wrong?

Plenty. "It was a dark and stormy night"? That's got to be the most clichéd beginning ever. The perfect story has to be original with something to catch the attention of the reader. It needs a hook that will make them want to read on. We want the reader to curl up with our story and lose all sense of the normal world. Start again.

Rebeccy came in through the cabin door, the glow from the fireplace turning her skin a delicious shade of honey. She inhaled sharply as Zebulon's gaze, almost physical in its intensity, probed every curve. But with her excitement came embarrassment. If only she had one of those store-bought dresses instead of this old burlap sack that her mother had stitched together a week after going blind. No matter, Rebeccy told herself. Her tight, lean body more than made up for the lack of good clothes. The workout sessions at Dan'ls gym in Boonesborough were really paying off.

Well, that's a *little* better. Great visuals, appeals to the senses, and has some neat atmosphere. It loses something around the gym part, though. Way too modern an element for that time period. Um, let's add an element of danger in the story.

"You're never leaving," the hunchbacked ogre with one eye and two teeth growled. "Your first mistake was running out of gas in

the middle of nowhere. Your second mistake was knocking on the door of this enormous, out-of-place castle in the middle of nowhere. Your third mistake was coming in after I opened the door and held the lantern up into your faces in the middle of nowhere. Your fourth mistake..."

Geesh! Okay, maybe not. How about some action? Everybody loves a car chase.

"There he goes! After him!"

"But I'm not done with my triple cheeseburger and monster dill pickle!"

"Look, you simpleton, that's the pervert who's been kidnapping all the puppies and kittens in the neighborhood and it's up to us to stop him. Now, get this hunk of junk moving or I'll have your badge!"

"Okay, okay."

McCullough tossed his food out the window and gunned the Corvette's engine, laying down a double rubber trail as they left the parking lot of Pick Your Own Burger.

"He turned to the right."

"Are you sure?"

"No."

"Great."

More rubber was lost as McCullough negotiated the turn. McMurphey was impressed. "Wow, great turn. Just like on TV."

"Thanks."

"Watch out for that moron slowly backing the huge truck out of that alley just as the crook goes by!"

"Hey, don't panic! I'll just hit the invisible ramp behind that old Buick over there and we'll jump right through his trailer."

The Corvette became airborne and lanced through the trailer like a hot knife through New York extra sharp cheddar cheese. It landed on the other side perfectly.

"Neat!" McMurphey shouted. "All that without one dent in my wife's car!"

"I'm a professional, man."

"Holy mother of all that's sacred! Watch out for that basket of puppies and kittens in the road!"

Stop.

What's wrong this time? It has it all. Action, cops, a car chase...

Yeah, it was good, but a car chase just isn't the same without video. Gunplay. We need gunplay.

Bullets flew like locusts, smacking into everything big enough to stop one. Dirk Buffman ducked as one punched through the barrel of toxic waste he was hiding behind. "Where's the blankety-blank helicopter?" he asked for the fifth time.

"That's the fifth time you've asked that," Shee Manwannabee hissed, firing a sustained burst from her sub-machine gun. Three more of Zortan's black-suited ninjas kicked their way into hell, or wherever it is that dead, godless ninjas go. "Can't you come up with an original thought, you hairless knuckle-scraping ape?"

"Hey, that's mean," Dirk replied. "Just because you're bigger and hairier than me, that doesn't give you the right to..."

"Shut up and keep firing! And try not to hit any of the puppies and kittens!"

Dirk ducked as an explosion ripped the air, the cake next to him disintegrating into a cloud of base elements.

"Right, that tears it!" he screamed, jumping to his feet. "Nobody crashes my birthday party and gets away with it!"

Hold it. We're on the edge of breaking one of our own sacred rules: never write anything cheap and gaudy.

Cheap and gaudy sells.

Sure it does, but I don't think we would enjoy it without our dignity intact.

I would.

Yeah, *you* would. Anyway, I read something the other day about war stories being really big now. Let's try that.

"Navigator to pilot, we're over the target, over."

"Roger that, over"

"Yes?"

"Pilot to bombardier, prepare to take over control, over."

"Roger that, over."

"Huh?"

"Pilot to bombardier, try to get the boxes on the target for once. Last time you spread puppies and kittens everywhere but where they were needed."

"Roger that, over."

"What?"

"Pilot to radio operator, notify the other bombers that we're beginning our run, over."

"Roger that, over."

"Okay, that's it, dammit! This is Roger That to crew. As of this moment, I'm changing my damn name."

Yikes, that bites. World War One, maybe.

Here I sit in muck up to my eyeballs, young Thomas wrote. *Oh, dear mother, living in the trenches is nothing like being home. Well, except for the smell. Every time the wind comes from the latrines, I'm reminded of the time Uncle Fartson blew himself and the outhouse up while smoking one of those giant cigars he loved so. Remember the fun we had trying to reassemble all the pieces?*

Man, that thought fell apart fast. You gave young Thomas a nice voice, though. Sophisticated, yet earthy. I still like the war idea. How about the Civil War?

"Damn Yankees!"

"Damn people that live in the south!"

"What? Why did you call us that?"

"Er, what would you like to be called?"

"Well, Sherlock, most people call us rebels."

"Okay. Damn rebels that live in the south!"

"No, no. You don't have to put the part about the south in it."

"Oh, I see. Damn people called rebels!"

"Just rebels, you pinhead. Just rebels."

"Damn just rebels!"

Bang!

Only you could turn the tragedy of war into a farce. Let's touch on the American Revolution. And, uh, try to keep a modicum of self-respect when you write, please.

"The Lobsterbacks are a coming, George!"

"Great, Martha! I'll fetch the butter and garlic!"

Thank you so much for listening. Forget war. Let's get back to basics. Perhaps the dawning of Time.

It was the dawning of time. The small band of wandering almost-humans had stopped for the night. They were frightened, huddled together around a pile of sticks they wished they knew how to light. They weren't used to being out in the open, but their caves were being fumigated for giant termites and...

No, wait, we had a glimmer there.

Since the earthquake, they had been seeking a place of refuge, any refuge to shelter them from the elements and the meat-eaters that plagued them constantly.

"Death to the meat-eaters!" Gooch cried around that night's pile of sticks. "And their ignorant persecution of us vegetarians!"

We're getting lost again. Try to stay focused, if you please.

Legend told of a far-away mountain slopping over with caves formed by a gigantic worm that had run out of giant apples to inhabit...

Um, let's move forward in Time just a tad, shall we?

"Ouch! What's that?"

"I call it fire. Ain't it neat?"

"No, it burns me up."

No, no, no. A little further forward.

"Ouch! What's that?"

"I call it electricity. Ain't it neat?"

"Shocking!"

Keep coming.

"Ouch! What's that?"

"I call it nuclear fission. Ain't it neat?"

"I'm glowing with excitement!"

I would have thought you'd realize by now that there's no story in inventions. However, if you would like to remain in the future, I suggest you lay out a little atmosphere and build a likable character.

The heli-bus settled to a smooth landing atop the Taco Gong building in downtown Fastfood City. As the passengers disembarked, a hungry Ralph Futuro looked around, taking in the hamburger conglomerates, the seafood emporiums, the Italian markets, the Hungarian booths, the Korean hovels, the Polynesian huts, the Japanese pagodas, the Chinese houses, the Thai restaurants, the French cafes, the British pubs...and blew his brains out, spraying the other passengers with blood, bone, and brains.

Ralph Futuro had a major problem with making up his mind.

Can you say "run on sentence"? Made me breathless just reading that load of useless drivel. Still, Science Fiction is very popular now. Let's try another tack.

"Oh, holy crap of Jupiter!"

"What's wrong, Glorp Ten?"

"I'm in big trouble, Bloop Fifty. I was just examining this human specimen and lost the little probe thingy. That's the fifth one I've lost this week! I'm gonna get fired, I just know it."

"Calm down. Are you sure one of the puppies or kittens didn't run off with it?"

"Positive. I lost it in...in...in there!"

"Oh, Teraxian dung! That human's gonna be walking mighty funny."

"I know and I've had my tentacle in there all the way up to the third elbow and—nothing!"

Man, how low can you get? I'm not putting my name to anything so steeped in low-life gutter trash. I mean really! How about something nice, soft, and literary? A mystery, perhaps?

Clothes were strewn all over the house, most still with body parts in them.

A mystery not a bloodbath. You know, like Christie or Conan Doyle.

Fog enveloped 221C Cooker Street. There was death in the air. You could smell it. You could feel it. And, if it wasn't for the fog, you could see it. The piles of murdered puppies and kittens were beginning to stink and...

What is this fixation you have with puppies and kittens?

I'm seeking an item to set the story apart. You know, a gimmick that compels the reader to read on.

Well, it's not working. In fact, *nothing* is working. Let's take a walk in the fresh air to clear our head. Perhaps some ice cream. Ice cream always helps us think clearly.

The soda jerk dug deep into the barrel of Irish Mocha Fudge ice cream and screamed as he lifted the scoop full of severed fingers.

Stop. We're not writing anymore. I'm turning off the lights.

Click! The power goes out, plunging them into darkness, the breathing of the horrible monster getting louder as their sense of sight is ripped away.

Stop it. Leave that keyboard alone, please.

He turns from the keyboard only to take an axe in the face, wielded by the maniac who had just escaped from the mental institution.

I'm not talking to you anymore.

The man mumbled and mumbled, for that was all he could do, having had his mouth sewn shut.

Stop! Stop it!

Dear reader, I'm afraid we're just butting our head against a wall. There will be no perfect story today. At least from us.

Please read on, though, and see the attempts by other authors, all of which are infinitely more successful than I have been today. Excellent, amusing, amazing, thought-provoking, and touching stories, all of which were winners in our first General Short Story Contest. We know you'll enjoy them.

"Enjoy this!" the captain shouted, firing all torpedoes at once.

Oh, shut up.

FIRST PLACE

WE COME TO SING
©2002 by Robert Paul Blumenstein

FROM THE CREST of the knoll, all the way down the ridge, the entire valley spreads out like a carefully smoothed blanket clean to the other side where the opposite ridge gathers like lumpy pillows. Only a crooked road creases the valley indicating that people have come back this far. And now, a plain white government-issued motor vehicle snakes along this road. Cecil squats on a knob-shaped rock, which slumbers atop the knoll, watching the car creep up the road. Even from this distance the wheeled box appears larger than a dinosaur. Faint echoes from rock and gravel thumping the car's undercarriage resounds as it grasps the mountainside beginning its advance toward the top. After the automobile ascends about two-thirds of the hill, Cecil runs toward a house that is situated on a plateau near even with the knoll.

"Hit's a comin'! Hit's a comin'!" the young boy cries. "That guvumint car's a comin'!"

His father leans against the porch post, cocks his head, and ciphers the sounds from the unseen approaching vehicle. He tightens his chin, twists it sideways, strokes his stubby week-old beard, and then spits into the yard. Gertie, his daughter, comes outside wiping her hands on her apron, her hair piled modestly on top of her head. A single strand of hair sticks to her sweating forehead. She brushes it back, and then gives her ear over to the distinguished sound of a vehicle traversing over their road.

Cecil pants, "They're a comin'! Paw, Gertie, they're a comin'!"

Gertie asks her father softly, "You reckon that's them? Do you reckon they kin give somepin fer Maw to make her better?"

He returns a reproachful hiss, "Stop frettin' girl! These guvumint people funny. Most of the time they say they kin hep you, but they always act like they a payin' fer it themselves. And then they give you all kinds of trouble..." He spits on the ground again, then focuses on the pass beneath the knoll timing the gravel clunks with the car's appearance.

A white Ford wearing a huge chromed grin bounces over the pass in the ridge and scrapes its bottom. The car drapes over the sides of the road as it slows to a stop in front of the house. The two women inside the vehicle glance at each other, then shudder as they scrutinize the house built on rock stilts fearing that it might slide off as soon as they enter it. Herman Compton, his daughter and son, Gertie and Cecil, and Uncle Harry and Aunt June carefully watch the women from their front porch.

"You reckon they afeared to git out?" Uncle Harry asks.

Gertie slips her arm into the crook of Herman's elbow and holds fast to him. "What're they doing, Paw?"

"Um huh um?"

Finally, the two ladies exit the car and shuffle toward the house. "That lattice work must have been a beautiful sight at one time. It's a shame to see it ruined," one of the ladies whispers to the other who flanks her closely after observing that the lattice underpinning to the porch has a few holes knocked in it.

The women bravely mount the steps and stand before Herman, who casually asks, "What kin I do fer you ladies?"

"I'm Mrs. Nugman and this is Miss Bridges. We're from Society Services. We're here to answer your claim for Medical Aid."

"Come on in," Herman enters the house without holding the door for them. The women hesitate, then enter the house. "She's in here."

A woman lies motionless on a bed in a room to the immediate right. Finally, she turns her head to observe the visitors. "What they want?" the sick woman asks.

"Mary, they gonna see if they kin git you a doctor, or some medicine, or somepin..." Herman says gently.

Mrs. Nugman steps forward, strains her posture erect, cocks her head sideways with a hen's vigilance to peck a cricket, and spouts, "No sir, Mr. Compton, this woman must come with us to be hospitalized, that's the rule."

The sick woman's face skin quivers as she struggles to voice her protest, "I ain't leaving you and Gertie. I'm staying right here with youins!"

"It's all right, me and Gertie are coming with you." Herman strokes her forehead.

Miss Bridges, a lead-bottomed woman whose eyes look like they could bend steel, steps forward and snaps, "Nu-u-u-u sirree! I'm the head R.N. at the hospital and we don't allow but one visitor at a time. And we have set hours for that. You can come Sunday. She either comes with us, alone, or not at all." The woman crosses her arms and poses like a wrestler waiting for the bell to start the round. The challenger, Aunt June, her strut undulating like the old goose that has been kept in the yard year after year for mercy's sake, hefts up two barrels of dark blue steel.

"Reckon if you guvumint people smart enuf to git up here, I reckon you're smart enuf to git out of here!" She and Uncle Harry defiantly sneer at the two women while glorying in their repossession.

Herman responds calmly, "I reckon, then, it's gonna be not at all. Now, if you two ladies will go back the way you came."

The two women visitors appear chalky pale, possess a peculiar indecisiveness, cautiously back from the room, and the dart through the front door.

Harry and Cecil follow behind June and shout, "*Git!* You guvumint garbage!"

Mary says, "Herman, I'm gonna die. You know that, don't you?"

"Naw-naw . . . Don't—" his eye sockets bulge a hot saline red.

"I'd die there in that old guvumint hospital anyways. That's no good without my people thur to say good-bye to."

"Naw-naw…" Herman's water breaks, tears stream down his face. He collapses on the bed clutching the inert mass underneath the covers and weeps until he falls asleep.

He vents all his frustration onto the old mule. This particular ground has not been plowed in several years. Many rocks have grown on this slope below the crest of the ridge. Plowing one of the lower fields would have been easier. It doesn't make much sense for Herman to plow this particular field, but he does it anyway. Earlier, Gertie called her father to lunch, but he chose to ignore her, and now he works on. His heart is empty. He hopes the strenuous work will empty his body, too, and lighten the weariness of waiting for his wife to die.

In the late afternoon, June and Harry stand on the front porch and observe all that Herman has accomplished. He's almost finished plowing the entire slope. The undulating furrows make the hill shimmer.

"That's pret' near four days work," Harry comments.

June ignores him. She looks beyond the field, over the knoll, praying that some omnipotent power remains at bay. Finally, fatigued from the struggle, she withdraws.

The sun sets, splashing the sky with a cool cerise purple. Suddenly, a hundred crows rattle the twilight with wings and voices shattering the quietude like delicate crystal. The flock comes about, then roosts in the solitary oak tree that grows on top of the mountain. The tree's patient tender buds will soon arouse and clothe the tree with lush foliage. Yet now, the tree can only offer the crows barren branches on which to lock their claws where they will sleep tonight. The birds ritually bury their heads under their wings, and then grow silent as ancient songs.

The spindly silhouette of Aunt June gracefully crosses over the freshly plowed field, undaunted by the lumpy furrows.

"It's time, Herman." Her gray eyes are sharp and clear, reflecting complete understanding of what is about to happen.

Herman stares at the crows, sensing that they have spoken to him. He intuits that it is time to go inside. He leaves the mule where it stands, then walks toward the house. A crow eyes Herman noting that his footing occasionally buckles under a clump of the newly turned earth.

Uncle Harry sits on the front porch watching June and Herman climb the steps. "Come in the house, Harry." He obeys her without looking at them.

Gertie and Cecil sit on either side of the bed. Harry and June take their place at the foot. Herman moves to the head and sits next to Mary. After a long silence, Aunt June finally speaks, "We've come to sing."

Mary mumbles a barely audible, "All right, then."

June speaks to everyone in the room. "As it has been for generation upon generation in our family, we come to the deathbed of our loved ones to sing so they kin go to God with a song on their soul..." She breaks into gentle sobs. Harry consoles her by clumsily stroking her hand looking like a man-dog laying a paw on a tiny kitten. "Oh, Mary, I'm so sorry that there ain't more of us here to sing..." Now, she weeps bitterly.

The sick woman lifts her head and says, "You are all my people, and you sing now, like you supposed to..." Mary collapses in exhaustion.

After a few minutes, Mary regains consciousness. She takes Cecil's hand and speaks, "Look at you. Still just a little boy..."

Gertie and Herman wince, registering reticent smiles. Herman tries to pacify Mary by stroking her forehead.

Mary lifts her head from the pillow and looks at the foot of the bed, "June? Harry?"

Gertie calms Mary back onto the pillow. "There, there, now. It'll be all right. Don't go on so, and try not to get upset."

"Herman? Don't forgit to go up on top of the mountain ever' winter to the clear spot where all the snow falls and makes a blanket on the ground. You know where I'm talking about?"

"Uh-huh."

Mary labors on, "Now do like we always done. Write all your worries in the snow, put them thur on the ground, write 'em in the snow. Just like we done ever' year of our lives. You promise?"

"Sure, honey, I'll do that."

"Are youins gonna sing so I kin go?"

Gertie opens the family Bible and flips to the back. She then sings from lyrics that Aunt June inscribed many years ago. Herman is unable to accompany Gertie.

Lord, send down your chariot now,
Wheels ablaze with fire.
Bright light laid on glory path,
Here's a soul for you to take.

Angels all gather 'round,
Lift this spirit from the ground,
Deliver her unto Jesus' hand,
Upon heaven she will stand.

Smile for us in the last,
So we may know it is coming fast,
We will walk with you as far as we can,
Seeing you go to that other land.

Mary lapses into unconscious, phlegm splatters in her throat, signaling her life's last moments. Finally, her head turns to the side and her neck goes limp like a bird that has smashed into a plate glass window. Her parted lips mirror subtle contentment shadowed by regret.

Cecil cries. Gertie lifts herself up and leaves the room. Harry and June slip from the room, too. Herman gazes at the dead woman for hours. Surely, she is only sleeping and will awake soon. He lies on the bed beside her and closes his eyes. His body is numb from the hard day's work, which helps him to drop off to sleep.

In the morning, he awakes well-rested. He rises from the bed and stretches. When he turns back to the bed, a life-razor cuts him at once when he sees his wife's face the putty wan color of the dead.

Harry enters the room wearing a frightened expression. "You all right, Herman?"

Herman can't answer him.

"We's afeared to wake you up, but warn't meaning no harm letting you sleep next to her all night. You know that, don't you?" Harry looks disheveled. He wears a yellowed tank undershirt and galluses suspending his oily work khakis. He cowers like a dog that is going to be whipped.

Herman wheels around in a spurt, which causes Harry to flinch. He then strides from the room and heads to the kitchen.

Harry follows Herman in a slow, methodic shuffle, shaken.

Herman sits at the kitchen table. Gertie cooks their breakfast on the stove. She casts an awry glance at him. Without looking at her, he passes his empty plate to her. His glare penetrates Cecil who sits across the table. His whole face is swollen as he munches on his breakfast.

Herman leaps across the table and squares with the boy, eye to eye. "When you git through stuffin' yer face, unhitch that mule out in the field and set it to pasture!" The boy is so frightened that he spits his food into his plate and scrambles from the room.

Gertie stares at her father in horror. "What did you do that for, Paw? Are you all right?" When he doesn't answer her, she adds, "Now I ain't got time to unhitch that old mule."

He merely points to the empty table with his fork. Gertie practically throws his plate of food onto the table. Herman flies from his chair and twists her arm behind her back, forcing her to her knees.

Like an evangelical preacher exorcising a demon, flame leaps from his protruding eyes, his face taunt with inspiration, he delivers, "I'll whoop the ever livin' daylights out of you ifin you ever do somepin like that again!" He then releases the girl. She scurries from the room wailing through an onrush of tears. Her father has always been gentle with her. This is the first time he has ever laid a harmful hand on her.

Aunt June has been leaning in the doorway ever since Herman came to breakfast. She moves fleetly from the doorway to the stove and pours herself a cup of coffee, then sets it down, unable to drink it. She sits down at the table with Herman.

"So, I reckon you got on your mind what you gotta do today, don't you? Ain't an easy thing to half to do, what you gotta do. Your paw pret' near killed hisself when he had to lay your maw to rest. But Herman, hit gotta be done and there ain't no hurtin' the one you love gonna make that burden any easier." As though completing a long journey, she pauses to locate her final destination, catches her second wind, then continues, "There's an old saying that we always say when we gotta do things we don't want to, even when it seems like it ain't quite right. It goes somepin like this, 'The cow's owner must git under her tail to push her out of the mud.' That's what you gotta do fer yer family, not beat 'em down when they need you the most, but git under 'em, push like hell and build 'em back up. Show 'em you kin be who you supposed to be."

Herman pushes his plate away not bothering to finish his meal and steps out onto the front porch. His eyes rake the hill to the top of the ridge where surely the oak tree still stands. He then fetches a shovel and pick and starts toward the tree.

On this day, the clouds meet the earth. Heavy drifts of moisture roll up the hill, waft through the tree limbs, and then tumble down the other side. The freshly furrowed field has turned to mud, which causes Herman's feet to weigh heavier as he trudges up the hill. Finally, he mounts the hill, stands under the great oak tree, and peers through the cradling limbs. He can feel the tree holding fast to the mountaintop, its taloned roots reaching far into the earth. This mountain has been Compton Mountain ever since Comptons came here. "Oncet, everywhar belonged to us," Herman mutters with contempt. Yet when he casts his eyes toward the valley, nothing but impenetrable fog glowers back at him, shrouding him in a cocoon.

Herman's pick drops limply to the ground wobbling to one side. He lifts it higher, strikes the earth harder. The pick hits a rock submerged just below the surface and careens off the ground giving his wrist a sudden twist. He grits his teeth while rubbing his wrist. He raises the pick high over his head and furiously drives it into the ground, repeatedly, until he tires. Herman examines the surface. His impetuous wrath is to no avail and yields nothing more than small round holes pierced in the soil.

Herman's clothes are soaked from the mixture of sweat and fog. He leans against the tree. His muscles burn from exhaustion. He looks up into the huge tree and watches tiny pellets of water cling to the branches, grow larger and heavier, and then fall to the ground. A scruffy crow with wet ruffled feathers lands in the top of the tree and sounds off commanding the clouds to part, and soon after, it clears as a gentle southwesterly wind blows the spongy air elsewhere.

Herman resumes digging. After he digs down a foot or so, the soil is less rocky. Yet, he soon becomes irritated with the impacted clay that sticks to his shovel. Inner frustrations grate on him. Usually, he tries to synchronize his inner and outer self. But the earth, which is twice as heavy as usual from water saturation, counters his body's rhythm. Soon, this enrages him and knots him thoroughly, inside and out.

Herman vehemently attacks the dirt digging more viciously than ever. He's annoyed that the shovel will not remove more dirt than it does. Next, the song comes to mind. He steadily grows enraged while he thinks about the atrocity of singing to a dying person. He remembers when his mother died. He was too young to sing, but nevertheless, he was forced to be present. He wheezes through his teeth thinking back on that occasion. The absurdity perplexes him more and more; why a room full of people would sing a song to someone who is fading away into the world of silence? He spits in his rage, groans and grunts, and digs more adamantly. Unconsciously, Herman hums in unison with his grunts. He hums louder and louder, digging with more vigor. Finally, he bursts into song booming out the same lyrics that Gertie sang to his dying wife sounding much like an opera singer. Suddenly, the hole darkens. Herman stops abruptly, aware of his singing. He looks up and sees several people standing around the grave.

"Come on out, Herman, hit's deep enuf," someone calls to him.

When Herman crawls out of the grave, he realizes that a small congregation has gathered to pay their last respects to Mary. While Herman was digging, Gertie arranged for Mary's coffin. The stark image of the crude pine box strikes out at Herman. He stares at it without moving a muscle; its oblong shape possesses him. The four pallbearers have to move him out of the way. They clomp through the mud and position the coffin over the grave, and then lower it into the muddy hole.

Harry gazes into the hole. Trying to console Herman, he awkwardly says, "You didn't hit nary a root. You're lucky."

Aunt June offers a eulogy. "Death passes like birth: With pain, with relief, and with quickness. We start raisen our younguns as soon as they're born, and so it is that we lay our dead to rest in a like manner. There was nuthin' to wait for, as waiting had alreedy been spent, and when the decided moment had come, waitin' any longer would have only prolonged the agony, producing nuthin' more than folly. She will lay now in the earth, nuthin' more kin disturb her, the pain of life is forgotten..." June trails off.

The preacher commences with the service. "Here we lay to rest our beloved Mary, who raised a family that to this day still holds to the mountain." A drop of water falls from the tree and lands on the Reverend's forehead. He looks up into the tree and catches sight of two sparrows. Several attendees cock their heads back, absorb their song, and watch the birds flutter from branch to branch chasing one another.

Gertie picks up a clod of earth and tosses it into the grave, which in the tradition of the clan ends the service. Now every person present picks up a clump of dirt to throw into the grave.

Not many folks came, only a dozen, all cousins. Each person studies the sticky, wet mud, speaks to it silently, before offering it to the grave.

June leans over to Herman and whispers into his ear, "Yer paw wouldn't throw no dirt. Somepin was lost that day. When you throw yours, try to remember."

Herman looks out over the valley as though to answer someone far away. He will be the last to throw earth into the grave, which will end the funeral. He picks up a glob of mud and squeezes it. It squishes through his fingers. He then shakes the sticky dirt from his hand onto the coffin.

Two cousins remain behind to cover the grave. Gertie and Herman stand to the side to watch them.

After a while, Gertie speaks, "Well, Maw is finally sleeping next to my brother Cecil."

"Yeah, she always wanted that, Gertie."

"I think she at last found peace up here on Compton Mountain with all her loved ones."

"I reckon so," Herman says without emotion. He is too exhausted to stand up any longer. He sits on a nearby headstone that marks the grave of his Uncle Harry Compton who rests by the side of his beloved wife, June.

A brilliant red sun hangs in the branches of the great oak tree. The red ball appears to inflate as a gust of wind passes through. The tree sways and drops of water rain to the ground as its tiny buds pop open.

About the author:

Robert Paul Blumenstein resides in Richmond, Virginia, where he was awarded an MFA in playwriting from Virginia Commonwealth University. He is a full-time writer having written not only for stage and film, but also has a published novel, *Flirtin' with Jesus*, the first book of The Ascension Trilogy. The second book of the trilogy will be released in 2002.

SECOND PLACE

THE INVITATION
©1999 by Frank Reynolds

"WHEN SINGLE WOMEN of my generation turned thirty, they didn't start frothing at the mouth and biting the furniture in fits of frustration." Gramma Bolger's staccato tone carried the piercing quality of a blackberry thorn. She edged herself forward in the big rocker, silencing its metronome cricking. "Thirty-five, I was, before I decided to hobble your Grampa, Lord rest him, drag him down the aisle and choke an 'I do' out of him." She tinkled the ice in her glass of lemonade and *tsked* her annoyance. "I repeat, at the risk of adding cretinous claptrap, patience has its rewards." Shaded by the eaves over the white-railed porch, she settled back to her rocking.

Angela Bolger shifted her kneeling position among the rose bushes. A brassy July sun burned the heavy Tennessee air into a shimmering haze, amber-tinting the seared hills beyond the whitewashed cottage and highlighting the colors of the myriad blooms in the small garden. A trickle of sweat etched a dark line down the back of her white sports shirt. She jammed her trowel into the earth between the plants.

"Patience!" Exasperation edged her tone. "I've been patient for too long." She raised her straw-hatted head and stared hard at the gray-haired figure swaying in the creaking rocker. "And you might as well stop carping at me. I've already invited Stanley. I'm cooking him dinner, and that's the end of that."

Gramma speeded up her rocking. "If he's anything like that dreadful little hemorrhoid you brought home last May, I'd spend a more interesting evening chatting with our neighbor's parrot. And the last dinner you cooked turned out to be about as appetizing as a pig's rear end."

Angela hid the hint of a smile and rolled her eyes heavenward. My only living relative must be the matriarch of all curmudgeons, she told herself. But I am fond of her, in spite of her rhetorical hand grenades.

She plucked a weed and threw it into the wicker basket. "I like this man. I'll marry him if he asks me."

"That's what you said about that Clarence fellow. Remember him? Hairless little maggot. One wheel short of a full wagon train."

"Clarence Cotter was kind, considerate, intelligent, and hardworking. You were too busy insulting him to notice."

"Congenital idiots are insult proof. A week married to him and either you'd have been the first in line to sign a petition to have him humanely put to sleep, or I would have sliced off the top of his head and spooned his brains out to the crows." Gramma softened her tone. "I'm just trying to advise you, child."

Angela stood, thumbed away a running bead of sweat from her forehead and brushed dusty earth from the knees of her jeans. "If you consider me a child at thirty-two, may I ask when you'll begin thinking of me as an adult?"

Gramma sniffed. "Perhaps a lifetime of teaching unprincipled brats at Eagan's Elementary has left my interpretation of maturity a trifle warped, but I swore to your mother, bless her ashes, I'd look after you until you were able to fend for yourself. Translated, that means discouraging you from marrying the first penniless numskull that takes your fancy."

Angela scuffed her way to the porch steps and sat in the shade. Gramma Bolger poured a glass of cold lemonade from the pitcher on the small table and handed it to her in silence.

The sun had reached its highest point, the white walls of the cottage fending off its heat, forcing the leaves of squash and zucchini plants into a wilting, protective withdrawal. The creaking of the rocker mingled with the drone of bees suckling at the borders of flowers. The soft clanging from the bell tower at City Hall drifted up the hill from the township of Eagan, wavering in the humidity, a mile to the east.

She can't bear the idea of my not being here, Angela thought. She's afraid. Afraid of spending the last few years of her life alone. Few years? She's eighty-five. Grampa lived to ninety-six. Bolgers past had longevity gripped in a headlock. Except my mother. Couldn't handle a simple childbirth. Why have I never hungered for her? Built-in anger because she never married? Resentment because I feel different from others? Latent animosity at being deprived of the security of my home and the love of my parents? "Your mother was born obstinate and died obstinate. She refused to listen to lawyers or to me," is all Gramma ever says.

Angela shrugged away the thought. "Anyway," she said, "tonight, when Stanley's here, I don't want you popping in and out of the kitchen clucking and tutting and throwing handfuls of seasoning into the pots when my back is turned." She reached for a brown-spotted hand and squeezed it gently. "And do try to be nice to Stanley."

Gramma held Angela's hand in both of hers. "I'll be as tactful as a politician at his own fund raiser." She eased her plump figure in the rocker until she faced her granddaughter. "I just want to see you settled and happy with the right man, and I pray continually to the good Lord to grant me that one favor. I know it's hard for a woman over thirty not to panic and start chucking herself at anything in trousers that resembles a male member of the human race, but believe in me, child, when I tell you to wait. I know the right one for you is out there. He will find you, or you will find him. Fate, they call it."

Fate brought me Stanley, Angela told herself, and I don't really care how you judge him. I'm truly attracted to him. Stanley has become a tangible part of my dreams. Stanley slips easily into my mental picture of a home, a husband, and children. Stanley is the one jigsaw piece missing from my life.

"You'll like him, Gramma," she said. "He's different."

"Hallelujah!" Gramma Bolger made the expression sound like a censure. "But if the specimens you've dragged to this doorstep so far are any indication of your tastes in the opposite sex, you'll understand if I remain perpetually braced for the worst."

"My tastes don't enter into it," Angela said, rising and heading back to the flower patch. "A solid relationship is based on mutual respect and an ability to give and take."

"That thieving little stoat you went gaga over three years ago had a one-sided notion of that theory, remember? Wanted me to shovel money into a scheme that would provide security for old me now, and for young you in the future. Disappeared like a ship in a fog when I suggested my friend, the district attorney, also might like to get in on the action."

"I'm not psychic, Gramma."

"No, but feelings of desperation make you easily led, child. Comes with the friends you insist on associating with. Like your school pal, Vinnie Allsop. Yo-Yo knickers, I believe, was her given name among village youths. Married that wart-faced shyster from the city. She thought he was Casanova the Second and that she was his volatile hormone bomb. Now the brainless little trollop finds she rarely has two quarters to rub together because her glue-sniffing disgrace to Homo Sapiens can't carry his dole payments past Murphy's bar."

Angela shrugged, using more vigor than necessary to trowel out a dandelion. "They've had bad luck. He's been temporarily laid off, that's all. Things will pick up for them."

"Hah!" Gramma slowly tilted the rocker forward, placed her thin white hands on the armrests and pushed herself upright, swayed for a moment, then shuffled to the verandah rail. The gold crucifix spinning from the fine chain around her wrist seemed to spark in the afternoon sun. The overly plump frame draped in a loose, white-collared black dress, the thick coarse hair fluffed like a miniature gray cloud, the austere, scrubbed-shiny look of features wrinkled like crushed parchment, gave her the appearance of a hatless mother superior. She peered through the sun's glare in a critical appraisal of the neatly kept garden. "Stop pottering around in that heat and come indoors. You're skinny enough as it is."

Angela waved a hand in reply and rose from the small foot stool she used when pulling weeds. She poked a forefinger into the neck of her white cotton shirt as she felt a bead of sweat run between her breasts. Firm breasts, she thought, not old breasts, yet. She inspected her hands, dirty from garden work, but still youthful, slender and supple.

What does Stanley see when he looks at me? she wondered. Does he see what I think I am? Tall, slender, good legs, passable features, nice brown hair with just a trace of gray. Is that what he sees?

Angela's pragmatic nature would never permit her to discuss with Gramma her feelings for Stanley. She could readily imagine the ease and the relish with which the old lady would shred and scatter in the breeze words like love and devotion and affection. Mentally she ticked off the facets of him that appealed to her. Stanley was lean, strong, and matched her five-feet-nine. He had a bulldoggish lower jaw that jutted when he felt he had something important to say. He treated her in a way she had come to need— with kindness and respect, salted with a little male authority—and he showed a fine sense of humor that ridiculed her concern that he was nearly six years younger than she.

"I'll make some tea," Gramma called.

As she watched the old woman disappear into the kitchen, Angela's glance took in the freshly stuccoed walls of the cottage, its dormer windows and dark slate roof, its green shutters and scalloped eaves. She smiled as she looked. She had loved the house and relished her life here. If only Stanley would consider making it their home when they married.

"I take it," Gramma said as Angela joined her at the kitchen table, "this Stanley is a fairly presentable piece of humanity. I mean, I couldn't keep a straight face for long if he turned out to be someone like that Felix Farber you used to date. His face had more dewlaps than an elephant's scrotum. They quivered so much when he spoke I stopped asking questions of him for fear he'd jar his teeth loose."

Angela grabbed at a paper napkin to smother a burst of laughter. "Felix was just a company client. I never dated him. My boss said he was interested in country houses. He was only here for an hour. I'm surprised you remembered him."

"With a voice that sounded like a toad farting in custard, how could I ever forget him? He had all the charm of a double hernia."

Gramma slowly put down her cup and looked directly into Angela's eyes. "Child," she said, "let's descend for a moment into the dark abyss of reality. It is obvious, even to someone blind in one eye and unable to see out the other, that you are convinced your future is tied up with this Stanley. I hear it in your voice, see it in the way you primp and preen every time you pass a mirror. If both you and he are sure of each other, then I'm the last person you must think of." Her old eyes roamed the stone-flagged country kitchen, lingering on the blue-enameled dishes lining the shelves, the immense cooking range, the shining copper-bottomed pots on hooks over the double stone sink, the white lace curtains on the multi-paned oriel window that looked into the garden. "This place is to be yours when I go, you know that. I can wait for His call just as well in Eagan's Home for The Aged. Besides, I've always longed to put a whizz-bang up the backsides of some of those elderly inmates who sit around the place like bunches of garden gnomes. Old folks need a little excitement now and then. Exercises the sphincter muscles."

Angela's hand slammed the table. "You'll stay with us, right here! Or you will sell up and move with us to wherever Stanley decides is the best place to set up home. No, no argument," Angela went on as Gramma's mouth opened. "And don't give me that

'I'll-be-fine-on-my-own' look. I know you will. But I need you, Gramma. I need that love you try to hide under a caustic veneer. I need to be near it every day. I need to feel it, hear it, embrace it. I need your presence to remind me that I have family I can love, to remind me that someone cares about me. I will not be parted from you." She felt her voice break, and she swallowed hard. "Look," she went on, aware her tone was almost pleading, "I know you will like Stanley, and he will like you, even if you are a back-biting, cantankerous, vindictive, lovable old she-dragon. Just meet him. That's all I ask."

Gramma nodded slowly. "Help me upstairs, child. Time for my nap."

In the evening, the heat had abated with the going down of a blood-red sun, the still air filling with the rasp of crickets and the scent of garden growth. Dishes rattled in the kitchen as Angela busied herself preparing dinner. Sipping on an iced mint julep, Gramma rocked silently on the porch, her eyes on the road that led from the town.

Angela heard the metallic mutter and the crunch of gravel as the small Volkswagen crested the hill and coughed to a stop at the garden gate. From the kitchen window she smiled to herself as Stanley, in dark suit, white shirt and striped tie, slid out, gazed about him quizzically, then pushed through the gate and up the path.

"Hello?" he sang out.

Gramma's voice cracked like a whip in the evening stillness. "At least there's nothing wrong with your vocal chords. You the young thug who's got my granddaughter smiling to herself all day like the Mona Lisa on Valium?"

In the kitchen, Angela winced. Shedding her light apron she took a step toward the kitchen door, then drew back. What quicker way to introduce Stanley? She watched his reaction from the window.

Stanley peered about him for a moment before catching sight of the shadowed figure in the rocker, then he grinned. "You must be Gramma Bolger. Angela warned me you were pretty forthright."

"Good. Then you won't mind my asking why a country boy is all got up like a pimp in a tart's parlor?"

"I'm supposed to make an impression." Stanley's grin widened.

"Hah! Another condemned soul crossing the Styx. Go tell Angela I said you're here. She's in the kitchen."

Still grinning, Stanley entered the house. He kissed a smiling Angela, who nodded with raised brows toward the porch as if to say "I warned you what to expect." She picked up a folding chair and led him outside.

"Gramma, meet Stanley. He'll keep you company while I see to dinner."

"Pleased to meet you, ma'am." Stanley stuck out his hand.

Gramma shook it. "Don't just stand there like a monument in a public park," she commanded. "Bend yourself into that chair. And don't call me ma'am. Call me Phoebe. I'm happy to have your company, if you can be bothered listening to one of the dullest creatures ever to break rear-end wind."

Stanley laughed. Angela sighed and shook her head. Gramma caught the quick squeeze of hands. She winked at Angela, who smiled and turned for the kitchen. That wink said a lot. Stanley had passed Gramma's first inspection.

"And bring us both a drink, child, unless Stanley is chairman of the local temperance society."

"Coming," Angela called back. She made sure the kitchen door stayed wide open.

"So," began Gramma, her sharp eyes appraising the resolute angles of the features of the man seated next to her, "Angela tells me you're a Tazewell man."

"That's right," Stanley said. "Born, raised, and went to high school in New Tazewell. Spent a few years in Knoxville, though. University."

Angela appeared for a moment to set down another julep for Gramma and a beer for Stanley. She kneaded him affectionately on the shoulder as she went back to the kitchen.

"Knoxville U," Gramma said. "Remember it well. The science teacher there had an urge to experience close encounters of the grubby kind with me in his office after class. I bit him on the nose. Angela studied there also."

"I know," said Stanley. "We had the same English teacher. Professor Orrin White."

"The idiot Chalky White?" Gramma exclaimed. "Pockmarked face? Looked as if someone had hit him with a hedgehog? Knew him when he ran around in those silly knickerbocker things. Hard to credit a clockwork ding-dong like him making professor."

Stanley smiled. "He retired a few years ago." He fumbled in his inside jacket pocket and produced a billfold. "This is my family and I, taken with Professor White at graduation." He handed Gramma the snapshot.

"How small the world is," Gramma exclaimed. "Never thought I'd see Chalky White's ugly mug again, except maybe on a wanted poster." She peered closer at the snapshot.

Monitoring the conversation from the kitchen, Angela acted quickly. "Dinner's ready," she announced, cringing at the thought of the caustic comments Gramma might make about others in the photograph. She helped the old lady up from the rocker and the three made their way to the large table set with white napery and shining cutlery.

Angela never felt happier. Gramma was at her wittiest, keeping Stanley in continual bursts of laughter at her scathing descriptions of some of Eagan's political aspirants, and on the senator for Tennessee in particular. "If his body matched his mind," she had concluded, "he'd be the invisible man."

When Stanley rose to leave, Gramma rose also. She insisted on accompanying them both to the car, forestalling Angela of a moment's intimacy with Stanley. As the taillights disappeared over the hill, Gramma reached out an arm. "Help me upstairs, child," she said. "I feel positively done in. Two juleps and a glass of plonk are too much for an old crone like me to handle."

"But you haven't told me what you think of Stanley," Angela began.

"A fine young man. Just fine." Gramma took Angela's arm in a tight, possessive grip. "But we'll talk in the morning, child." She turned toward the stairs. "In the morning," she echoed softly, her old shoulders more stooped, her shuffle more labored.

She knows, Angela told herself, stealing a glance at Gramma's solemn face, maintaining the silence between them as she led her along the hall. She knows Stanley and I will marry soon, and she's afraid, but this time it's my turn to be strong. Angela opened the bedroom door and leaned to kiss a wrinkle-webbed cheek. "Goodnight, Gramma," she said softly.

Closing the door, she leaned against it for a long moment. It will take time, she assured herself. She'll come around. She likes Stanley. It's the change she resents. In a few months . . .

An odd sound insinuated itself into her thoughts. She pressed her ear to the door. Gramma's cough, she decided, frowning. No. Wait. Sobbing? Softly she turned the handle and eased open the bedroom door.

Gramma, kneeling at the foot of the bed, her hands joined in prayer, had her eyes fixed on the framed picture of the crucified Christ above the dresser. The tears that wet her cheeks were left to run.

"Why, Lord?" Angela heard her whisper. "Why make sure I saw that snapshot? Must I fragment her dreams of love and motherhood? Must I dash to smithereens her last glimmer of future happiness by telling her that her chosen partner in life was sired by her mother's lover?" She swallowed, stifling a sob. "You know well, Lord, I must."

Angela started toward her, arms outstretched, but already she felt an ever-tightening, breath-robbing constriction begin in her chest, and she knew that in a moment her heart must surely burst.

About the author:

A Scotsman, Frank Reynolds taught English and Italian at colleges both here and in Europe. He writes a Scottish History column for a British magazine, and edits a college newspaper. He moved from the San Francisco area to a cabin in the Sierra foothills in 1995, where he tutors English and Italian professionally at the local college, and writes whenever he can.

THIRD PLACE

SOLDIERS AND DANDELIONS
©2001 by Tessa Jones

THE SUN RIDES high, at its pinnacle, shining down bright and hot on a cloudless, windy day. I keep my head down low, stepping off the sidewalk into a sea of sand surrounding the lone bus bench. The brisk wind whips the grains of sand into a stinging fury, attacking arms and the backs of legs. Eyes half close against the onslaught, each grain finding its way through my eyelashes feeling like a boulder, massive and heavy. My hair tosses in the stiff breeze, becomes a careless tangle.

I sit down on the weathered wooden planks of the bus bench and wait. Another blast of wind and I bow my head against it, tasting grit in my mouth.

My slit eyes catch yellow movement at the juncture of bus-bench leg and ridged-up sand. It's a dandelion, nestled amongst fluttering jagged leaves, yellow head bobbing on a skinny green stem. *Dent de lion.* Lion's tooth. Noxious weed, according to some. To me, a beautiful flower. Hardy, too, growing in the middle of well-kept lawns, seas of sand, the sides of roadways, even in the cracks of sidewalks. Or at the feet of bus benches.

I slide off the bench, crouch down and touch a thin yellow petal. My fingers tremble. My mind skitters backward, whirling, to a younger time, and the fingers touching the dandelion become chubby and soft and clumsy.

The sun disappears and the wide, little-kid smile turns to an O of terror as a man looms over me. Daddy. I feel him jerk me to my feet, and as he drags away my struggling body, he flattens my beautiful dandelion with a careless foot. Cringing, I stare up at him. Fear. So much fear. And after the fear, pain. He whispers to me in a thundering voice. *(Be a good soldier.)*

My heart drums in my chest as I return to the present. It's hard to breathe. Tears trickle slowly down my face. Glancing around, I see that no one else is at the stop, and none of the speeding cars seem to have noticed me crouching in the dirt, touching a dandelion wedged at the concrete base of an old bus bench.

I sigh with relief, and start to get up, but another blast of wind sends the yellow flower twitching and bobbing. A shift in the mind, and I'm nine years old, staring out the bedroom window, tummy growling, oh so hungry. Legs heavy, feeling like dead wood nailed to my hips. Day twenty-four without food. A test from God, Daddy says, to see if we are good soldiers. And in the unkempt back yard, dandelions spring up in riotous clumps of jagged green leaves, bright yellow flowers, and white puffballs ready to explode in the springtime breeze.

A giggle brings me back to the bus stop, and I see a tangle of white and green and blue. A little girl in green shorts and tee-shirt, her hair a cloud of short blonde curls, clinging to her mother's jeans. The little girl is staring at me, amused (look at the funny lady, mommy.) The mother, I can tell, is *not* so amused.

I try to get up, so I can dust myself off and appear somewhat normal, but I just don't have the energy. I sink back down on my heels, squatting there, yet another slide of my past slipping into my viewer brain. *Click.*

Daddy going through his "dark time." Again. His broken mind dips into the pit of hell. Reads a sign from God, written in veins across his own forehead. God gives him his instructions. He reaches for me, and I cry out. *(Be a good soldier.)* When the fear consumes me, and I can't breathe anymore, Tracker comes.

Tracker, a strong, tough, young man. Grim. Tracker reads signs, too. He sees Daddy tracks. Tracker never smiles, but he knows how to get through the things that Daddy does to us. He's brave. Fearless. He plucks a dandelion and puts it in my tiny hand, and sends me off to sit on StoryTeller's knee. The fear and pain ebb away to nothing as I bury my nose into velvety-soft petals and listen to a story of long ago and far away and once upon a time. When the story ends and I come back, I wonder at the soreness, the smell, the bruises. And where's Tracker? I look for him but he's nowhere to be found. I miss my friend. Even if he *doesn't* smile.

Two sharp blasts from a car horn and I'm back at the bus stop. My knees are stiff from crouching in the sand. The blonde, curly-headed child still with her mother. The mother looks at me strangely, and shields the child from me with her body, as if afraid that I might hurt her. I laugh at the thought, but it turns to a sob somehow, strangling in the back of my throat.

Hurtling back through time, I'm hiding behind *my* mother's legs, wanting to disappear while the monster-daddy hunts for me. He is close. I can smell him. I hear the belt slide whisper-soft through the loops of his pants, and mother steps away, giving me to him. No, mommy, please. *(Be a good soldier.)*

Suddenly I'm in the deep end of a pool. I can't swim, and terror washes over me as a large daddy hand grabs the top of my head, pushing me under. I thrash my chubby legs and my tiny hands try to push the weight off the top of my head. My lungs burn for air. As he yanks me up by my hair, I hear his maniacal laughter, and the words "baptism." I do not understand. I gasp and choke. *(Be a good soldier.)*

Again at the bus stop. I take several deep breaths, as if to reassure myself that I can indeed breathe. The little girl cries at the sand blowing in her eyes. I look up and whisper, "Be a good soldier." Mother and child move to the far end of the patchy sand, close enough to run to the bus when it arrives, far enough away to be out of reach of the wild-eyed, tangled-hair woman squatting at the base of the concrete bus bench, muttering while she fondles the petals of a many-bladed flower.

(Be a good soldier. Be a good soldier. Be a good soldier.) It echoes through my head and I wonder—a good soldier? What is that? A soldier kills or is killed. What's so good about that? Why did Daddy always insist upon it? I shiver in the hot sun, and watch idly as the wind blows and a dandelion seed from a puffball floats in from somewhere far away, a tiny parachute delivering a seed of life to this dusty Texas town.

It lands close by my dandelion, and I push a few grains of sand over it to hold it still. A partner, I tell the flower at my feet. It nods its yellow head in gratitude.

A squeal of brakes startles me, and as I look up, I see that the bus has come. The little girl and her mother are already boarding. I rush to get on. One single backward glance reveals the dandelion, standing tall and tough in its blustery, sandy world. I climb the steps, slip some change into the slot of the metal box. As I make my way to the back of the bus, I stare at my lone dandelion through graffiti-scratched windows.

As the bus pulls away, I'm sad for a moment at the loss of my dandelion. But then a voice whispers to me *(Tracker, is that you?)* and says, "Don't you get it? *You* are the dandelion."

Me? *I* am the dandelion? The understanding ebbs and flows for a moment, my mind a tidal pool. Then I grin. I stomp my feet. I throw my head back and laugh. *Me.* Yes. *I* am the dandelion. I am strong. I am tough. I am even pretty to some.

Then I get mad. I yell in a fit of rage, "Daddy! Can you hear me? Listen up! You can try to destroy me. But you can't kill me. My soul runs as strong and tough and deep as the roots of the dandelion. I will survive. I *have* survived."

I laugh again, and pound hard on the vinyl seats of the bus. I notice that everyone has shifted, moving to the front, vacating the entire back of the bus (look at that funny lady, mommy.) Oh, dear.

Off the bus, and into a tall building, all glass and steel and fluorescent lights. It's dim and cool and quiet inside. I ride the elevator to the third floor, fidgeting until the doors whoosh open. I run down the hall, burst into the office and blurt out, "I may not be a good soldier, but I'm a damn good dandelion."

My shrink, with his carefully schooled, blank face, just nods his head and says, "I see."

About the author:

Tessa Jones, originally from Miami, Florida, has been fascinated by the human psyche for as long as she can remember. Along with "Soldiers and Dandelions", Tessa has also completed a novel entitled "Fragments", a psychological thriller about a woman with Dissociative Identity Disorder (formerly called Multiple Personality Disorder). She is hard at work on her second novel, "Redemption", about a female serial killer. Tessa has previously sold one short story, "The Weaver" to an online publication.

THE ABDUCTION
©2001 by Jennifer K. Antonacci

I FEEL NOTHING. Well, shouldn't say that because it isn't completely true. Sometimes I feel like I am from another planet. I continue to pace back and forth until I feel a dizzy spell coming on. The loud pinkness of the walls in my room is screaming in my ear, provoking a sick and twisted feeling in my stomach. The thought of actually drinking Pepto Bismol makes it worse.

"This is the ugliest damn room I have ever seen," I snap to myself as I stare at Fuzzy Bear. That's all I ever call him. I ripped the eye off when I was nine, but he was always precious to me. Maybe it is time to give him to Goodwill.

I lie down on my bed to take a little break, even though it isn't well deserved. The clock on my end table reads 8:31 pm, but time is of no use to me. Professor Hermanns wants this short story assignment entitled 'My Best Talent' stamped by his secretary by nine tomorrow morning and I don't dare think to ask for an extension. "Only God gives extensions in life," he preaches. I expect to hear these words at least twice a week. He also says that everyone has at least two talents in life, but most people get so wrapped up in the first one, "Their head's too far up their ass," to see the second. Writing is my first, and it appears that writer's block is my second. I throw my bear across the room and it hits a hanging picture of a sunset I took a couple of years ago. I can't remember where. I watch it fall, but the bang still makes me jump when it hits the ground.

"Screw you," I mumble to the clock as I turn it around to face my pink wall. If I have to stay up all night, then I will. I can usually bang these stories out within three or four hours. I say 'bang' because I know people whose stories take them three weeks to write, and that's based on group effort. My friend Dom always has his mom write the outline for the beginning of his story and his dad the end. He says that not only does it get his assignment done, but it also reassures the parents that they're "helping their son." It also gives him a better glimpse of what his parents are really like, when they're not thinking like parents.

Something has to make sense soon, or else I am going to go crazy. The *green* dots on my clock seem to be blinking right in my face. Is it me or has that clock grown in the last hour? Anyway, Professor Hermanns is always one step ahead of everyone else. His syllabus is based on an exact schedule with the day the story is due and what its topic is.

Writing is the one ability I have in life that allows me to step into someone else's shoes when I don't feel like tripping on uneven pavement anymore. It is the one thing that gives me a sense of control in the world because I, and only I, decide how I want the elements to look, smell, and feel that day. Me, myself and I call the shots. Give me a call if your boyfriend is cheating on you and you want to seek revenge.

8:34. I think about all of the fiction novels, autobiographies, short stories, poems, newspaper articles, student compositions, anxiety and depression pamphlets in my doctor's office, encyclopedias, TV Guides, magazines, Dr. Seuss books, and every other piece of reading material ever written. I wonder how they do it. Why do those people get to be authors and I don't? Do they go through this too? Probably not. Every one of them must be a genius. It's the only explanation. It's amazing how many thoughts can cross your mind in just seconds. 8:34 again.

I wonder if there is an old 'Speak and Spell' lying around in the basement somewhere. "Idiot, that won't help," I bark. I know my letters, just not my words. I have no ideas, but I do have a blank computer screen. My brain is numb and the loud environment, which, strangely enough, I haven't noticed until this very moment, suddenly irritates the hell out of me. Why is it that the family pisses you off the most when you can tolerate them the least? To make matters worse, the same outer corner of my left eye has been twitching all day. I don't care what anyone else says; every academic class in college will make you sweat at one point or another. I have friends who say that college is easy. Of course it is when you sleep through class and then constantly borrow notes off of your roommate. They take the easy way out and do well, while I study and still look like the fool. Night sweats are my only way to cope. They are my "Well balanced diet, while getting plenty of exercise." They are detox to my mind, body, and soul.

"A $28,000 college education is *supposed* to make you sweat." This is my father's favorite line. I get the feeling that he pictures his paycheck on my forehead every time he drops that bomb on me. When I was a freshman I told myself that it was because the "daily sacrifices" took my parents some getting use to and that these little undeserved guilt trips would calm down. Now I'm a junior, and it's like no time has passed at all. I'm just the middleman between my parents and the Bursar's office. It's all merely an experiment to see if I am worth the money. Maybe I should drop out and be a bank teller. At least then I'd be getting paid to be in the experiment.

My head suddenly jerks towards the door due to the stomping I hear below. Once again, the anarchy continues almost exactly as it had yesterday, and the day before, and the day before that. It begins with my mother yelling at my seven-year-old brother, Dylan, for something. Last week it was over him setting sticks on fire with a magnifying glass. Now his latest thrill is throwing pieces of cheese singles on the dog's back just to watch her twirl around in a frenzy looking for the scrap, while all along it's stuck to her like glue. When she finally does figure it out she rolls around on the ground to get it off, inhale it, and wait for some more. He laughs and keeps doing it until my mother walks into the room, again, to discover his devilish antics, again. He then runs downstairs to the basement knowing damn well that she won't go down there due to the pig sty which is a "site for sore eyes." This is the escape route, no matter what the crime may be. It is actually pretty funny to watch, but I bet the Crocodile Hunter would even find it annoying today. My other brother, Ryan, is a senior in high school and isn't home that much. Rumor has it that him and two of his friends blew up the mailbox down the street with a cherry bomb. Can you see the family resemblance?

To make a long story short, the whole episode finally ends with, "Wait until your father gets home, little man," his laughing echoed by her yelling. Can you believe that his grammar school has a great reputation in town? Man, Oprah would love us.

8:49. The two green fluorescent dots on my clock blink 60 times per minute. That damn clock is stalking me. My blank computer screen is making me drowsy, so I don't want to sit. When I stand up, though, I pace back and forth and that makes me dizzy. 8:49 again.

"Think, damn it!" I yell to Fuzzy and I stare at the blinking cursor, again. My corkboard is more interesting. It contains paraphernalia of past events in my life. My eyes pierce these items like needles. They start with the pictures from high school of my two best friends and me making pig faces in one of those tacky picture booths on the boardwalk in Wildwood. It continues on with fortunes from fortune cookies, which I kept as a form of self-therapy. Then there's the Allman Brothers concert ticket stub, not inspirational—priceless, my 'first time donor' sticker from the Red Cross last month, the picture of me proudly sitting on my blue bike with the training wheels when I was five-years-old, a piece of garlic gum which my friends tried to get me to eat once, a list of quotes which I look to for a sign for what's in store, and the pressed rose I took off of my grandmother's coffin last December. Yet, out of all that, the cursor blinks on. It actually has the nerve. My life is a sham.

"I need to get out of this room," I blurt. I slam off the light switch. I can't think anymore—period, even though I am not sure if I started to in the first place. The sharp pains in my lower back really kick in as I fly down the stairs. How does Santa do it?

"Cheap K-Mart chair," I grumble. I can't get comfortable whether I am standing or sitting. For some *strange* reason, I have a flashback to the time last year when I had to drive to the airport by myself to pick my father up from a business trip.

As I munch on Doritos (I hate the WOW kind) and slurp Diet Coke, I realize just how hungry I am. I forgot to eat dinner. I've overheard sorority chicks in class say that while they exchange drunk tales from the night before. They probably don't eat on purpose just to leave more room for their "just make me something fruity" drinks. I always get a good laugh when listening to them talk about the drunk-dial phone calls (a.k.a. booty calls), which they "promise" themselves they aren't going to do, again. I'm sure the no-one-leaves-until-every-pledge-pukes-at-least-once frat guys are well worth the calls, too. They do take their schoolwork seriously, though. Just the other day I heard two different sorority chicks plotting on how they can avoid reading that 500-plus page book for a boring Art of Ireland class and still get at least a B on the paper. Of course, everyone knows that Ireland is such a boring place. I think it's safe to say that their parents' $28,000 tuition has its work cut out for it.

I can hear the fam shifting throughout the house, but they are nowhere to be seen. My mom is downstairs surfing the Internet for Christmas gifts. What is that site again? Oh yeah, www.shoot-me-now.org. My father and my brother are doing their usual ritual of watching TV together. One night they are in the family room, and the next the living room. Sometimes they stay in one room more than one night in a row. There is no pattern to it or reason why. It is just their thing. Tonight, it is back-to-back episodes of The Three Stooges. Tomorrow it will probably be a movie on TNT that has been played in every other time slot for the last two days, which they've probably already watched. It's always one of those movies that you find yourself giving the remote a rest to whenever you stumble onto it, even though you've seen it a million times. This week it's The Ghostbusters. Does that define quality bonding time, or what?

As much as I dread it and would do anything to avoid facing my writer's block, I have to get some words down. Maybe I can even form a paragraph. Hell, at this point, one or two pages would be an act of God in my book. Right now, any idea would do. There's a bar in town called The Brownstone that has this huge, wooden bear mounted in an upright position, right in front of its doors. Well, someone keeps chopping the poor thing's hands off right below the elbows. I know it's not real, but I still can't help but feel sorry for it. The funny part is that when the owners replaced the appendages the first time this was done, someone (I'm assuming the same people, probably teenagers) did it again. The owners gave up, so now every time you pass that corner in the middle of town, you unmistakably see a large, upright, wooden bear with a severe handicap. Now *there's* the basis of a plot that could make a ridiculous mystery story. It has a boyish sense, doesn't it? I think I'll leave that one to the Hardy Boys to figure out.

In the past, ideas came to me so fast that even my 60-plus WPM typing skills couldn't get them down fast enough. I was a bottomless pit in a glutton's body. I was unstoppable. Now look at me. It's not like I left this until the last minute. Writing assignments are the one thing that I actually look forward to. I have been tackling this project for the last week, with one dead end after another. I already lost my virginity, so this surely isn't entitled to sleepless nights.

My family history is a cornucopia of ideas, but deciding on a place to start is like trying to catch a wild turkey. I can tell you stories that would make you roll, though. Debbie, my mom, is five-feet-zero and a.k.a. Little Debbie. This story is so damn funny, that every time she tells it she laughs just as hard as she did the first time. It's her favorite from when she was about ten-years-old. During a "once in a blue moon" lobster dinner in the middle of August, her father decided that the satisfaction didn't end with the completion of the meal. He took the empty lobster shells and put them all over the backyard. Then he knocked on the Polish lady's door across the street to warn her of the Special Report he had just heard on the giant bugs that were invading the neighborhood. The poor thing didn't know whether to keep beating them with a broom or save herself and take the next boat out. Mom, Nana, and my Aunt Kathy laughed so hard as they spied through the front window, that they almost peed their pants. Leave it to the Irish to be the ones laughing.

My father, Vinny the Guinea, as we like to call him (and just a little part of him likes it too), comes from quite a different background. This will give you a good idea of what I'm talking about. My grandmother's idea of dinner for a family gathering on a Sunday afternoon was heating up Kentucky Fried Chicken. Sal is my father's brother and both he and Dad always dragged all of us along just for the sake of keeping the family unit together. It was more like a blueprint of a unit. To think of it, I don't even know what one would look like in order to attempt to design a blueprint of one. Whenever I was there, I always had the uneasy feeling that something big was going on that the adults didn't want us kids to find out about. It wasn't uncommon for yelling matches to break out, specifically between my father, uncle and grandmother. It was during one of our "Griswold get-togethers" that my uncle first expressed his extreme disapproval for Agent Orange. I often wondered for a long time what that was and what it ever did to him, but not anymore.

9:06. "Where is that piece of paper with that line I jotted down from yesterday?" I had asked myself this yesterday, too. "Remember what your main idea is here, Jen," I tell myself as I pass the full-length mirror. I think I actually repeated this line in my dream last night, when I was lucky enough to get that one hour in. Ooh, dreams. They always have good stuff in them. "I think I've become my own best friend," I say as I slowly lose the battle to keep my head away from the pillow.

I feel clammy and cold as my eyes try to focus. The framed

sunset still hasn't risen yet.

"What the hell?" It is the only thing I can think of to say. I am not completely awake yet. I feel hung over, even though I haven't been drinking. I sit up and try to gain consciousness. Then my memory downloads like America Online to my desktop. I squint as a beam of light shoots right at my pupils. Why the hell is there light at nine o'clock at night? I look to my clock like a fifteen-year-old looks to the little stick-that's-more-blue-than-pink, which she has been trying to get herself to look at for the last two hours. Please tell me that what I am seeing isn't true.

6:27 am.

I search my brain for some kind of logical explanation. How the hell could I have possibly slept through the night with out being woken up at least once? How come the phone didn't ring? Do people know about my new best friend? How come I wasn't asked to empty out the dishwasher? Is it because Ryan had used all the dishes for target practice? What the hell is this, some kind of joke? There is no way that I am going to make my deadline. I am screwed. I am completely screwed. Can it be true? Maybe I really *am* an experiment. Part of me doesn't even recognize myself. For a minute I can't even remember who I am. My blood feels different, but I didn't know it was even possible to feel my blood flowing within. I can't feel my tongue, but the words come anyway.

"*Something strange and green is doing this.*" I am between the worlds of REM and reality. I see little men before me. I must still be dreaming. No, I'm just losing it. REM ends and reality begins. Suddenly, I know in my gut that I am not crazy. It is all so clear. It has nothing to do with my distractions and dysfunctions. My life has nothing to do with me at all. I am in the hands of something beyond control and prediction. I have been abducted by aliens. That's why my brain is mush: they took it, poked it, altered it, and put it back.

Now *there's* a meaty story idea for you.

About the author:

Jennifer is a 1999 graduate of Villanova University with a BA in Human Services and a double minor in Psychology and Sociology. She grew up in Wyckoff, NJ and now resides in Hoboken, where she commutes to her Human Resources position in New York City's World Financial Center. Jennifer discovered an interest in writing in the third grade when she turned a simple writing task into something much more than was expected. She was warmly applauded for her efforts by the reading teacher, but still had to redo the assignment.

MISS WILLA WEMBLY
©2001 by Bettye D. Grogan

I LEFT MY home on a brilliant June day to drive the hundred or so miles or so to visit my parents back in my hometown. The late spring flowers were still in bloom and freshly tilled fields gave off a familiar aroma as I drove through the country. I felt a growing excitement as I neared Millersville. I always got that feeling when I went back home, even though I had been gone for twelve years. Somehow there is a sense of having never left, of going back in time when that town, that place on the map, was the only spot on the planet.

I drove slowly around the town square. The front of the drug store had been remodeled, but the hardware store down the street had the same ragged awning on the front. There was a new name on the dress shop; Miss Helen must have finally retired. The Confederate cannon still stood guard over the small park in the center. It was a pretty little town. I smiled as I circled the park twice. As a free-lance writer with three growing children, my visits were infrequent, and I didn't often take time to notice the changes.

I wound around to the old corner house where my parents lived and pulled up to the curb. The white house with its green shutters was beginning to look run down at the heels. The paint was peeling badly under the eaves, and the green front door had faded from dark to light. It was too much house for my parents with so much upkeep. I worried about them climbing the stairs, since they both had arthritis. But any discussion about change met with stony silence.

Dad met me before I got to the door and greeted me with a bear hug. He seemed thinner, a little frailer.

"You are an early bird! We didn't expect you before ten o'clock."

"Dad, you know I get up at five-thirty every morning. I couldn't sleep any later if I tried."

I returned his hug and noticed how rounded his shoulders had gotten. He wasn't an especially tall man, five-feet-ten-inches or so, but had always been ramrod straight. I am so much like him with the same dark eyes and steely gray hair, only mine was covered up via Miss Clairol in a honey shade I hoped looked natural.

We went straight to the cheery yellow kitchen where Dad already had our cups on the table, and a still-steaming coffeecake sat in the middle. The air smelled like cinnamon and reminded me of the Christmas cookies that my grandmother used to make each year.

"Mother is still upstairs getting dressed," he said as he started toward the coffeepot.

"Let's wait for her," I stopped him, and we sat down in the worn ladder-backs. He reached for my hand across the yellow plaid cloth.

"You look great. How are Bill and my beautiful grandchildren?"

"Fine, Dad. I know you are disappointed that I didn't bring them, but three children arguing in the back seat just wasn't my idea of a fun day. I needed some time off, for a change."

"Well, we're always glad to have you to ourselves once in a while." He patted my hand as my mother swooped down and hugged me over the back of my chair, pressing her cheek to mine. She looked younger than her years with her bright white hair and beautifully made up face.

"Did you see what I made you?" she nodded proudly at the coffeecake. Mother never liked to cook and I knew what an effort it was for her, so I praised her offering and hoped that it would be edible. Surprisingly, it was. She cut me a large piece and we filled our cups and settled down to talk.

I caught up on all the gossip and the illnesses of cousins, the births of twins in the neighborhood. Two of my old classmates had become grandparents already, which blew my mind since I was just getting my three all in school at the same time. What a late bloomer I was!

Of course, there were several deaths since my last visit. An old neighbor of Mother and Dad had lost a battle with cancer. Dad slid me the paper and I thumbed through the pages of local news of people I no longer knew. I paused to read the obituaries. Then I saw it at the bottom of page two, the obituary of Miss Willa Wembly.

"Miss Wembly died," I said, almost to myself.

"Yes, she'd been ill for quite some time, but didn't let anyone know. She still took her dog for his walk around the block every day right up until she became bedridden. She was ninety-three," Mother said, smiling. "She never told anyone her age, you know. I don't even know how they found out for the paper."

Miss Wembly was an artist. She made her living with her art and doing genealogies and coats-of-arms. She was a woman ahead of her time in that she was single and quite independent. She evidently loved her unmarried state and signed all her work "Miss Willa Wembly" much to the amusement of the town, most of whom thought her very eccentric. With her long dresses, beads and sandals, she was a hippie before such were heard of, a women's libber before that identity was born. But a kinder, warmer person would have been hard to find.

The old dial phone on the kitchen wall broke my reverie of Miss Wembly. It was Mrs. Southby next door asking Dad to come and help her get her husband out of his bath and dressed for the day.

"I'll go with you and take them some of this cake," Mother cut two large pieces and wrapped them in foil. "They will be so glad to see you, Rebecca."

"Mom, if you don't mind, I'd like to take a walk and work out some of this stiffness from driving. I will run over and visit before I leave."

They walked across the street and I headed down the block in the warm sunshine. The Foster's house was spectacular with azaleas, and I paused to take in their luscious colors. At the end of the block I turned and walked down by the old houses, many of them over one hundred years old. Some were stately, some were getting seedy-looking with neglect. I soon found myself in front of Miss Wembly's house.

It was very old, square and tall, the brick crumbling, paint peeling badly on the porch. The house and the low stone wall around it went back to the Civil War, so said the plaque just outside the gate. On impulse, I pushed open the creaking iron gate and walked through high grass to the garden in back. I remembered her garden, so lovely with flowers and herbs. To my surprise, it looked the same. The flowers were mulched nicely, and peonies sent their sweet perfume over the herbs. I remembered how she had loved mints, and there were several kinds. I pinched one and sniffed lemon mint. I reached for another and crushed it between my fingers—pineapple mint.

Sitting down on a small concrete bench, I thought about Miss Wembly of twenty-seven years ago. I was thirteen when invited to one of Miss Wembly's teas. Four of my friends and I wandered through this garden, dressed in our Sunday summer dresses before going in to tea. Miss Wembly told us the names of all the flowers and let us pinch the mints and guess what flavor each was. Then we went into the coolness of that old house to her dining room, set with chipped and mismatched china, but adorned with bouquets of flowers. At each plate she had made a little nosegay laid on top of a small coat-of-arms that she had painted, especially for us.

We felt so grown up to be there having tea with Miss Wembly, and to be given a gift of her own hands made us feel so important. She told us, individually, what each family emblem meant. Then she poured the tea and served us tiny cakes with great flourish. In the dimly lit room with its well-worn old furniture, we felt like we were having tea with royalty. She, with her salt and pepper hair pulled back in a knot and her print dress from the same pattern she always wore, attended the big lace covered table like a queen.

Her dog, in those days, was Shelton. He was a mutt that she got at the pound, but she treated him like he was a son. She introduced him, on her walks, to strangers and regaled old friends with his latest cute trick. We all got a kick out of Shelton who had no idea that he was a dog at all. At the tea that day, I can remember trying not to giggle as Shelton settled by my feet, bare in sandals, and proceeded to loving lick my toes throughout the whole tea ceremony.

The back door slammed and I jumped as I saw a man with a cane locking it behind him. When he turned, I realized it was Mr. Starks, the president of the bank and an old friend of Dad's.

"Hello, Mr. Starks," I rose to meet him.

"Rebecca! How good to see you. You look wonderful. Your dad tells me that you stay busy with those lovely grandchildren and your writing and don't get home often."

I felt guilt seep into my heart, and I looked at his cane, thinking of a reply.

"The cane? Knee replacement. Had the other one done six months ago. This one has taken longer to heal. Let's sit down and talk a bit." He dropped with a sigh on the bench and I sat beside him. After asking about his family and telling him about mine, I asked about Miss Wembly.

"I have looked after her affairs for years. You know, she lived just above poverty, and I kept things repaired as best I could for her. When she became ill, she never said a word. Took that walk every day just like she always did. It must have worn her out."

"Who kept her garden? It looks like it did years ago."

"She did, up until the very last. Then the neighbors pitched in and kept it. She lay in that big old bed and looked out the window at her garden every day. That's where I found her, her dog laying right beside her."

"Shelton," I said, smiling.

"Oh, Honey, Shelton's been dead for years."

"Of course," I said embarrassed.

"She got another dog from the pound, named this one Andrew. Treated him just like she did Shelton."

"What happened to Andrew?" I asked.

"He's at my house. He's old and almost blind, so I figured that we could keep him until he goes. She would want it that way."

I moved closer and slid my arm through his. "You were a good friend, Mr. Starks. I wish I had taken more time to visit with her these past few years."

"Well, she was a good friend too. She brought pleasure to everybody. Always giving away her paintings to friends and having teas for you young girls."

"Did she still do that?"

"Right up until the last few years when she got weaker. She felt like girls enjoyed dressing up to come to her tea parties. And I think they did."

"Oh, yes, we did. I went to several, but I remember the first one most of all."

"Well, Rebecca," he rose with an effort. "It's been good to see you. I must get home; my wife will wonder what has happened to me. Hello to your parents. And don't be a stranger. Come by and see Edna and me sometime. We're retired now. With our children and grandchildren so far away, we get awfully lonesome."

I opened the gate for him and watched him limp away, remembering the vital athletic man he used to be. Then, knowing my parents would be wondering about me, I closed the gate, said goodbye to the beautiful garden, and continued around the block to my old house.

I found my parents still in the kitchen. Mother was already thinking about lunch. As she surveyed the open refrigerator, I suggested that we go out to eat. Her face brightened.

"I'll get my purse." She almost skipped up the stairs. We drove out of town to a new restaurant that they had wanted to try. Its rustic decor was charming and the food was good. We met several old friends there and, of course, Dad passed around pictures of the children and Bill and me. Then we visited some cousins that I had not seen in years. I was amazed at how much they had aged.

On the way home I told my parents about going to Miss Wembly's. Mother remembered me dressing up for the tea parties, and had thought it amazing that I would willingly shed my jeans for even an afternoon.

"I wish that I had saved the coat-of-arms that she painted for me. I would love to have that now."

"You do have it," Mother smiled her bright fuchsia smile. "I saved it. It's upstairs in the bureau."

As soon as I parked, she went up and brought it down to me. The frame had tarnished, but the colors were still bright.

"What a gift she had," I said to Dad. "She could have gone somewhere else and made more of her talent, surely."

"Of course, she could. But she loved living here with her dogs and friends and her garden, I guess. Life is not always better if you get famous and rich. She had everything she wanted right here."

The afternoon went by fast and too soon it was time to leave. After the quick promised visit with the Southbys, I gathered my purse and keys. Mother put the coat-of-arms in a sack along with coloring books for the kids. They walked me to my car, and I gave them both an extra-long hug.

"Come more often," Dad whispered. "Your mother misses you."

Mother stuck her head in the window and gave me another kiss. "Hurry back," she said, as she always did.

The drive home seemed short because my mind was recalling so many things that had happened to me in that little town. I was sorrowful that so many things had changed, that my parents were aging, that old friends were dying. But I felt glad, too. Glad that friends still helped friends, that small town neighborliness was alive and well. I vowed as I sped down the four lane that Bill and the kids and I would spend a weekend a month with Mother and Dad. They would need us more and more. And I wanted my young children to see old houses, old cousins, roots from which their mother sprung. I wanted them to see Miss Wembly's garden.

As I approached my house, I began to make plans. Bill could take our son on a fishing trip. He had been talking about that, but just hadn't had the time. And I would have a tea party for the girls and their friends. I would get out the best china and put nosegays at each place. I would wear a long print dress and lots of beads. And I would hang my coat-of-arms over my computer to remind me of my heritage, my family . . .and Miss Willa Wembly.

About the author:

Bettye D. Grogan is a native Kentuckian, is married, a mother of three, and a grandmother of seven. She and her husband, both recently retired, stay busy with gardening, church, community activities, and (most important to Bettye) she now has time to write! Bettye also belongs to state and local writing organizations. She wrote her first story at age eleven and has since written books for children, poetry, songs, and a short novel. Bettye thanks her Hoptown Writers colleagues for keeping her enthused and writing.

DIARY OF A SEDUCTION
©2000 by Charity Tahmaseb

NOVEMBER 1

Dearest Anne, I've instructed my lawyer that, in the event of my death, he's to forward this package to you. My last request is you read these pages before passing judgment—on either of us.

Reginald

JUNE 15

I've found her.

Sitting innocently on the main patio reading, of all things, Chekhov, she was well in the shade of the umbrella. I straddled the chair next to hers and said something witty, something along the lines of how customs should have confiscated her tome and required reading at the resort is Jackie Collins.

She smiled so I asked her name.

"Anne."

In a sea of Ambers and Tiffanys, her simplicity was refreshing, the sarong and tank swimsuit enticing in their modesty. Her voice was crisp, like white sails snapping in the wind. The thought drew my gaze to the bay.

I nodded toward the boats bobbing in the water. "Have you been sailing?"

"I don't know how."

"I'll take you."

"I couldn't . . .I mean, I don't know you."

A slight blush started at her neck, then flooded her cheeks. I watched, fascinated, and held out my hand. "Reginald."

I chatted long enough to confirm my initial impression of Anne—an early dinner, followed by a reasonable bedtime, then up early for some sort of exercise.

My first instinct is to "bump" into her at dinner, share a table, wine, and close dancing. I've ordered room service instead, relishing the anticipation. She's the one—and to think I almost didn't come this summer. The routine had become predictable. There's no chase left in the chase, no thrill to the hunt.

But with Anne I know the pursuit won't be easy, it might not even be successful. That alone makes me want it more. For tonight, I'm content to scribble across cheap hotel stationery while pondering the attack.

JUNE 16

She *would* choose something beastly like jogging. I slipped the pool boy a hundred pesetas, and he showed me her route, which I immediately rejected. Tennis racket in hand, I decided to find an early morning opponent, when Anne nearly collided with me on the path to the courts.

"I don't suppose you play," I said.

"A little."

"Up to a match?"

She pushed stray curls from her face, then gathered the mass into a ponytail. Her eyes on mine, she nodded.

A little, indeed. I may never be able to show my face on the courts again. But if I'm a poor loser, then Anne is gracious in victory. Besides, I'd gladly lose a dozen matches for another lesson in the art of elegant and effective backhands. She stood behind me, so close her proximity raised the hair on my legs. Our hips align, although she stands several inches shorter than I do.

But she couldn't reach around to grab my wrist, so we switched and I embraced her, followed her movements, and I'll be damned if it won't help. Still in my arms, she tilted her head to look up at me. I gave my most reassuring smile.

"Thank you."

"Sure." Her lips were slightly parted, inviting, but it was far too soon with someone like Anne. Instead, I suggested breakfast.

Tonight, I did bump into her at dinner. Nearly missed her as she stood, to my surprise, at the bar, chatting with the bartender. Her eyes lit up when she saw me—a mixture of delight and wariness. I paid her tab, although I'm sure the bartender planned on doing the same.

"Friend of yours?" I asked, nodding toward the man who noisily served patrons at the far end of the bar.

"He's a nice man."

I chuckled. "There are no nice men here. Present company included." Slipping my fingers around the stem of her wineglass, I added, "So, have dinner with me?"

I watched, again fascinated. Mirth in her eyes warred with the solemn expression she tried to affect.

"That," she said, "would be nice."

Anne, I discovered over dinner, speaks three languages, teaches Russian literature, and saved for two years to take her trip.

"It was spontaneous," she said.

"Spontaneous? I'd hate to see how long it takes you to do something planned."

She giggled. "The destination was spontaneous. Once I had enough money, my travel agent sent me suggestions until I saw one I liked."

"I'm predictable. I come here every year."

"So I gathered."

I raised an eyebrow and watched the flush spread across her cheeks.

The waiter, along with our entrees, interrupted my plans for further inquiry. Not until we were sipping brandy on the screened porch did I raise the subject again.

"So, why here?"

"It sounded so exotic and romantic—I couldn't resist."

"Then dinner must have been an extreme disappointment."

"Oh no. I—" The wariness crept into her eyes. In her gaze, I watched the private battle wage—practical Anne against her "spontaneous" self. The blush turned crimson. "Not at all," she finally whispered.

The lights from the club flashed and sparkled. I almost suggested dancing. But the thought of the noise, the banal gyrations, the appalling lack of intimacy left me lethargic. Anne deserved better—so did I, for that matter.

A marble chess set, the color of cotton candy, sat between us. In all my years vacationing here, I've never seen anyone use it. I scooped up the queen. "Do you play?"

"A little."

"Good Lord. If it's anything like your tennis game, I'm in serious trouble."

We played until we reached a draw by mutual agreement. A sudden yawn wracked Anne's body and sleepiness gave her a childlike glow.

"I've kept you out too late." I offered my hand. "May I walk you to your room?"

Her hand slipped into mine and we walked in silence to her "garden view" room.

I didn't press my advantage, although I sensed I had one. Her warm, sleepy mouth drew me close, but my kiss was chaste, brotherly. Anne gripped the knob. The brass rattled in the doorjamb as we said our goodnights.

I tell myself to take this slow—a woman like Anne is worth it. The victory will be all the sweeter for the wait.

Yet, now that I'm alone in my room, I wonder. Instead of finding Anne, perhaps somehow, she's found me. The game has suddenly become a great deal more interesting.

JUNE 18

With charm I'm growing increasingly susceptible to, Anne lured me beyond the manicured lawns of the resort, up a rocky path I'm sure only mountain goats should travel, to the bluff overlooking the sea.

"What do you think?" She spread her arms wide. "Isn't it beautiful?"

"Breathtaking," I said, my eyes never leaving her face. My reward—the blush. Anne blushes a great deal in my presence, and I search for ways to keep the pink in her cheeks.

A grassy knoll beckoned, and somehow, I maneuvered her on her back. Blades of grass poked through the spirals of her curly brown hair. She's beautiful and I told her so.

The wariness has almost left her eyes, yet sometimes it sneaks in—as it did then—just around the edges.

"Anne." I had to know. "Are you afraid of me?"

"Maybe I should be."

"Why?"

"Miguel says you're trying to seduce me."

"Miguel?"

"The bartender."

"Of course," I muttered. A dozen different thoughts swirled in my head—the main one involved having the man fired. My habits are well known at the resort, as is my money—generally neither is questioned.

Instead, I asked, "What do *you* think?"

Her eyes sparkled with mischief. "You're a cynic with a lousy backhand."

I burst out laughing, she joined in, and the sound echoed around us. A spasm constricted my chest, and I hacked, my laughter choked off in a sudden stream of coughing.

"Reginald, are you all right?"

"Fine, fine. It's all this clean living. Nothing a pitcher of martinis whipped up by your friend the bartender won't cure."

We headed back down and had those martinis, or at least I did. Then we spent the night together, outside, side by side on lounge chairs. To my amazement, I learned Anne can identify all the constellations.

"I was going to study astrophysics, be an astronaut."

"What stopped you?"

"Freshmen year in college, I fell in love."

I raised myself on one elbow. "Really?"

"With a mad Russian. Three, actually. I changed my major—doubled in language and literature."

"So, who won your heart?"

"Chekhov because he's sad, Pushkin because he's tragic, and Lermontov because he's a cynic."

I burst out laughing, bringing on the cough. When I felt a hand on my shoulder, her body next to mine, the rush of gratitude conquered my embarrassment.

"I'm sorry."

"What for?"

To cover for an answer I didn't have, I urge her forward until we shared the chair. With Anne in the crook of my arm, I pointed to the sky. "Which one's that?"

She glanced at me, expression curious. "You mean the Big Dipper?"

"Assume I've never seen the sky before."

She giggled, then gave me an astronomy lesson that sounded more like poetry. I made her repeat the names over and over, until her voice grew sleepy.

JUNE 20

Convinced Anne to go sailing with me. She brought her camera, snapped pictures of the rugged cliffs that line the cove, other boats floating in the bay. I stayed out of range, but it was a futile gesture—she never pointed the lens in my direction.

It's better that way. Photographs have a knack of showing up when you least want or expect them. Still, call it male ego, I wish she had at least asked to take my picture.

Anne signed up for snorkeling, but I backed out, blaming the sun's glare on the water for a massive headache. If I didn't have one before, I do now, after spending the day sulking in my room. Images of Anne have plagued me all afternoon. Why I chose not to explore the bay with her is beyond me.

It's too late for dinner service and I've no doubt missed Anne. Footsteps passing my door make my pulse jump, but I'm invariably disappointed. I will try again tomorrow. A tennis match, perhaps. I could do with another backhand lesson.

JUNE 21

Before the match even began, I held up my arms in defeat, brandishing the racket. "I'm a hopeless case."

"I don't know about that."

Lessons before, instead of after, for this game, and Anne pronounced me fit to play. And play we did. She was the victor, though not for my lack of trying. I approached the net, anticipation coursing through me.

"Good match." I tracked a bead of perspiration as it slipped down the side of her face.

"Yes."

Handshake to hug, and our skin met through the corded squares of net. The sensation made me ache for her and we kissed—hot, slick, and salty. Had I been sixteen, I would have fainted. As it was, she stole my breath.

"Oh!" Anne broke away, flushed, a trace of wariness lingering in her eyes.

I tried to reel her in, but she protested.

"I'm all sweaty."

"So's what I have in mind."

Announcing my intentions, albeit crudely, had a strange effect. The air cleared, yet clouded between us. Anne's smile turned alluring, a look I've seen on many women, but never with such dazzling results.

Perhaps because the game is new to her, or I'm drawn to her "spontaneous" self, but I'm convinced this will be the most wonderful affair of my life—the one I'll treasure when arthritis claims my joints and I can do little more than bore those around me. I eagerly await her next move.

JUNE 22

Caught Anne in the boutique today. Since the shop only carries thong bikinis and lingerie, I was curious what practical Anne would find there. From the window, I watched her hands skim the rack of silk nightgowns. She lingered on one—the color of pale champagne—and I applauded her choice.

I crept from behind as she held the silk against her body.

"Wear it to dinner."

She jumped, and the blush arrived with a vengeance. "I don't think they'll let me wear it into the dining room."

"My room, then. At seven." I touched her cheek. The skin nearly burned my fingers and I felt, more than saw, the nod.

JUNE 23

Anne sleeps in my bed. And here I sit, scratching out words by the sliver of light from the bathroom, where I've spent the last two hours.

Clever, clever girl—she wore a robe as though headed for the pool. The terrycloth lays crumpled by the door. We ate on the balcony, toasted with champagne that matched the silk. Little conversation—the inevitable was on both our minds.

I reached across the table and brushed the curls from her face. The wariness has left her eyes, replaced by a look I've never seen reflected back at me. I traced her cheekbones, ran my fingers over her lips, her eyelids as though the expression were a mask I could wipe away.

She sighed. The sound made my chest constrict. I choked back the cough.

The bathroom became my refuge, and my biggest regret is I've needlessly alarmed her. After thirty minutes, she tapped on the door.

"Reginald, are you okay?"

"Fine. I think it was the Paella." Thank God for fish.

"I'll call the front desk, ask for a doctor."

"That won't be necessary." Even as I said it, I was hit with a fit of coughing. The doorknob rattled.

"Please let me in."

"I'm fine, really. Why don't you lie down? I'll be out in a bit."

I paced, ran the shower, avoided my image in the mirror until certain she'd be asleep.

And she was, with a worried frown on her sweet face. As I write, I steal glances at her. The sheets do little to hide the athletic form. The strap of the gown flirts with her shoulder cap. God, I long to kiss her, even in sleep. But that's cheating, and with Anne, I can't do that. I will confess all in the morning.

JUNE 24

Anne has left. I watched while she scanned the front of the hotel, eyes shaded by one hand, as though searching for something lost. With one last look, she stepped into the taxi.

My feigned stomach upset has become a reality thanks to drinking most of yesterday. Not even with strong coffee would the words come, so I ordered a pitcher of Bloody Marys and found courage in vodka. I sat her down, took her hands.

"I'm married."

She looked pointedly at my left hand and her fingers slipped from my grasp.

"I don't wear a ring," I added. More accurately, I don't know where it is. "I'm sorry. I didn't mean—"

"Don't say it." She shook her head so the curls bounced like springs. One spiral hit my cheek—the caress lingered long after she tamed the strands.

Her gaze drifted to the bed, then back to me, her eyes painfully hollow. "Thank you for not . . ." she broke off and looked away.

"Yes." It was all that would come, for I had no defense. Poor sweet Anne who names stars and falls in love with dead Russians— I knew, didn't I? I knew from the start. Smart as she is, in her mind love and marriage are irrevocably linked. And a cynic doesn't love.

Always the gentleman, I helped her into the robe, knotted the belt, then found I couldn't let go. I wanted the look to return, aware that in my grasp I simultaneously had and lost everything.

"Anne."

"Reginald, please. Just let me leave."

I honored her request. After everything, how could I not?

JUNE 25

Asked the concierge to find me a copy of Chekhov. The man gave me a blank look, so I added, "He's an author."

"Of course, sir. I'll see what I can do."

Three hours later, a cabana boy delivered a volume poolside. The cover is well worn, the spine creased—a true book lover's book. Notes fill the pages like secret correspondence from one reader to another. It occurs to me this is Anne's book.

JUNE 27

Called Sutton and asked him to start divorce proceedings, prenuptial and consequences be damned. He advised against it, of course. Then suggested I cut the vacation short, see a doctor about the cough. Perhaps he's right.

JUNE 28

Climbed the path Anne and I took. After the coughing subsided, I laughed. Good Lord, perhaps tomorrow I'll challenge myself to a game of tennis.

Games. The word makes my face burn with shame. I pray the little games I played with her leave no lasting scar. As practical as she is, I believe Anne knows how to heal herself. Or perhaps I only hope. The universe has far too many stars that still need names.

I'm running low on hotel stationery and it's this more than anything that's prompting me to leave. Ridiculous—I can always ask for more. But folded in half, the sheets tuck nicely into the volume of Chekhov. Now that Anne is gone, I have little to say.

The idiotic thought that if I could return the book to her, show her these pages, she'd—not forgive, that's asking too much—but perhaps she'd understand. Would she smile at my fumbling attempts, like she had at my pathetic backhand, then show me the way?

Before I leave, I'll take the boat out one last time and listen for the snap of her voice as the wind whips the sails.

And for what it's worth, dearest Anne, my backhand is still lousy.

About the author:

While working fulltime as a technical writer, Charity Tahmaseb also writes short and long fiction. Her first published short story appeared in the April 2000 issue of Futures magazine. Her story in the December 2000 issue of Futures placed third in their "Fire to Fly" contest and was recently nominated for a Pushcart Prize award. Charity lives in Minnesota with her husband Bob, son Andrew, daughter Kyra and Dalmatian Toby.

ROAD RAGE
©2000 by Miller Chandler

THERE WERE SEVERAL advantages that came with growing up on a main highway. Having to pick up trash from the side of the road was not one of them. A weekly duty of mine between the ages of thirteen and eighteen, I hated that disgusting chore with a passion. That did not deter my dad from making me do it, however. He felt that it built character. Besides, it was good for the people driving by to see the young Chapman boy out picking up garbage. It made me seem like more of a regular fella in the eyes of the country folk.

We were a very well-to-do family for our small Middle Tennessee town. Dad could have had me out picking up trash, chopping logs, or digging ditches with my bare hands, for that matter; I still would have been perceived as a "rich kid." My father was a self-made man, and people respected him for that. He knew, though, that people were not going to respect me just because I was his son. He knew, if anything, it could make things harder for me.

There was one time I went out to pick up the road frontage that I will never forget. It was early November during my senior year of high school, and I had gotten my hands on two tickets to the UT football game. My buddy Jake and I could hardly wait. All week long, I found it even more difficult than usual to concentrate on my studies. College football is like a religion in the South, and we were two faithful followers. Before I left for Knoxville, though, I had to take care of my chores at home.

It was unusually cold that day, so I bundled up in several layers of clothing. I wasn't even to the end of our driveway before my ears and hands started going numb. As I started walking along the highway, it was as if I wasn't wearing any clothes at all. The wind from the oncoming traffic cut right through me.

There was a strip of grass about fifty yards long on both sides of our driveway outside of the three-rail fence. It only took a few days for this area to get covered with a pretty fair amount of trash. After a week, it looked downright—well—trashy. People threw out bottles, bottle caps, cigarettes, cigarette wrappers, cans, fast food and chewing gum wrappers, and anything else they felt the immediate urge to discard. Once, I had to pick up what appeared to be a used condom with a stick I rounded up from the yard. Why someone would be driving around with such a thing is beyond me.

I was finished with one side of the drive and had started on the other, when I heard what sounded like a rather loud truck drawing near. I didn't give it much thought, at first. I just kept on walking, only stopping to pick up more garbage. I bent over to grab a crushed can, and I heard the truck accelerate. Now it had my *full* attention. I straightened up and turned just in time to see an object coming straight for my head. There was no time to react. It struck me, and I was out cold.

I am not sure exactly how long I was out, but I think it was only a couple minutes. When I came to, a strange man was kneeling over me. "Can you hear me, young feller?" he asked. I could hear him and I told him so.

"There's something in my eye," I said to the man. He told me not to worry and asked me if I lived in that house over yonder.

He walked me up to the front door, and my mother answered—hysterical. "Oh my God, he's bleeding!" Mom screamed. "What happened to him?"

"I don't really know, ma'am. I found 'im a layin' on the side a the road in a pool a blood an' broken glass. Looks like somebody went an' threw a bottle at your boy's head. We'd better get 'im ta the hospital, ma'am. It looks like he's lost a good bit a blood."

The man looked to be about sixty. He was haggard looking, but with kind eyes. He wore old faded jeans, a dirty white T-shirt, and a John Deere cap. I figured that he must be a tobacco farmer.

He told Mom that he would follow us to the hospital. They loaded me in the car, and the last thing that I remember her saying before I passed out again was, "he looks so *pale.*"

She called Dad on the way there, and he arrived not long after we did. As soon as he showed up, he took complete control of the situation. By this time, I wasn't even speaking in complete sentences, but I could still sense that he had taken charge.

Hugh Chapman was the best athlete that ever came out of Robertson County, Tennessee. After high school, he went on to become an All SEC fullback at UT. This is where he met my mother. She was the head majorette. Dad built the most successful courier business in the Southeast from the ground up. A loyal staff of hundreds admired my father, as did every man that played alongside or against him. And then there was me.

I wasn't as athletic as he was. I was a pretty good high school football player, but not good enough to play college ball. I didn't inherit his movie star good looks, or his naturally great physic. And I was never better than a B student in school. Basically, I was the average son of a small-town god.

I never resented him, though. His intentions were always honorable, and it was painfully obvious that he loved me. And when I needed him the most, like that day I just about bled to death on the doctor's table, he was always there. I admired him just as much as everybody else did.

I must have been nodding off while the doctor was trying to sew me up, because the nurse kept putting this awful smelling stuff under my nose. I didn't even notice them put the IV in my arm. There were many tiny pieces of broken glass embedded in the layers of skin on top of my head, and they meticulously removed every last one of them. It took over twenty-five stitches to get me patched up properly. The doc said that the impact of the bottle gave me a pretty good concussion, and that I would probably be a little foggy for the rest of the week.

As I rested on the emergency room table, I listened to my father and the farmer talking on the other side of the curtain. Rusty Cobb lived on a plot of land by the Bagget farm, and had worked for the family for the past thirty years. Dad told him that he went to school with Jo Bagget and asked him to please tell Ed he said hello. I heard Dad thank the man, and he replied with, "If you'd been in my shoes, youda done the same thing."

I rode home with my father and there wasn't much conversation between us. We rode along quietly with only the faint sound of country music playing on the radio. I could smell the smoke from his cigarette, despite the windows being cracked, and it was comforting to me. It felt safe.

I was home only a short time before he asked me, "What exactly happened out there today?"

"I'm really not sure, Dad. I turned to look behind me when I heard the truck speed up. I only saw the bottle for a split second. Then I was out."

"Did you see who threw it?"

"Well...Dad, I'm really not sure."

I think he had a feeling that I knew who did it, but he didn't press the issue. He asked me if I needed anything, and when I told him no, he left me alone to rest.

The truth is, the night before the bottle incident I made a terrible mistake. I went for a walk, to my car actually, with a girl named Darla Handley. We had been talking all night by the bonfire at Joey Donohoe's party. She asked me if I wanted to go someplace where we could be alone and, without hesitation, I said yeah.

Darla was a pretty, buxom blonde that went to East Robertson High School. I'd had a crush on her that dated back to kindergarten, but I always assumed that I didn't have a chance. She had gotten in a fight with her boyfriend, Johny, earlier that night, and he had gone off with the boys. He had cheated on her countless times, and she was on to him. She would get her revenge through me.

Our rendezvous in the car was fairly innocent. We kissed a lot, and we talked. Mainly, she just needed a friend. I knew that she wouldn't break up with Johny. He had her wrapped, and everybody knew it. Still, I was willing to risk my life by being seen at the party with the girlfriend of the toughest son-of-a-bitch in the county.

I did enjoy embellishing a bit when telling the tale of Darla and me to my friends. After all, if I was going to almost get killed just because I messed around with some girl, I might as well make it sound like it was worth it.

A week passed by, and the doc turned out to be right; I was still a little foggy, but I was getting better all the time. When Dad asked me to clean the road frontage, I just sat there and stared in disbelief. I didn't mean to be disrespectful; I was just literally in shock. I guess I thought he would just hire someone to do my chores from then on. After I had been traumatized so, how could he expect me to go back out there? When I finally snapped out of it, I told him that I would do it after lunch.

That day, the traffic seemed worse than I had ever seen it. I got a crick in my neck from turning my head every time I heard something louder than a Honda. I was nervous as hell the whole time I was out there, but dammit, I *did* it. It actually felt good to face my fear, and get back out there. It felt good to pick up trash!

After graduation, I decided not to go to college right away. Instead, I joined the Marine Corps. Going back out on the highway so soon after the incident had changed my life. On that day I discovered what an incredible rush conquering fear could be. And there was no room for fear in the Marines.

I was in Guantanamo Bay, Cuba when I received the news of my father's death. He had a sudden heart attack at the age of fifty-one. I was granted a leave to go home and be with my family. His funeral was on a rainy Sunday in the Spring. That was always his favorite time of year.

It was years later when I found out what a rough morning my father had back then as well. Mom and I were talking about him the night of the funeral, and she told me that he just about wore a hole in the carpet, pacing the floor as I picked up the road frontage. She said that he chain-smoked cigarette after cigarette while watching me through the living room windows.

Dad taught me several important lessons that aided me in being a good Marine and an even better person. He taught me to be a hard worker and to give things that are important to me my all. He taught me to never quit. And he taught me how to be a good listener. He would have been proud that I chose to attend his Alma Mater after I left the Corps. He always assumed that I would.

There is one thing about my dad that I did not know while he was alive. He was not a man without fear, as I always thought. There was something that completely terrified him. He could not stand the idea of his only son getting hurt. And watching me in pain, as he did in the hospital that cold November day, was something that he never got over.

About the author:

Miller Chandler is a certified personal trainer at Belle Meade Country Club in Nashville, Tennessee. "Road Rage" is his first submission for publication.

THE ARTIST'S STUDIO
©2000 by Jessica W. Hench

NORTH BROAD STREET lies between Clay and Main Streets in downtown Salem, within a mile of Roanoke College. It is the length of one block. On the west side of North Broad Street is the Salem Farmer's Market. It consists of a long, wooden counter running the length of the street, and turning the corner onto Main Street. The counter is a few feet wide, and has a roof over it. A sidewalk runs parallel to the long counter. A copper weathervane sits atop the Market on the north end of the roof.

On the east side of the street are a few buildings. The two-story brick building on the corner of North Broad and Main Street is a small antique shop. The windows display winter decorations: snowflakes, a Christmas tree, and soft lights, giving the store a country cottage look. The entrance is on the corner of the two streets. On the side facing North Broad Street, there is a single window. Past this window, in the same brick wall, there is a white garage door. It is unlit inside, but peeking through the windows, I see shelves with boxes and tools, and in the middle of the room, a large piece of heavy equipment. There is a white door to the right of the garage. This entrance has a window on the upper half with a sign on it advertising the sale of an artist's studio on the second floor.

I often walk down North Broad Street on my way into town to stroll down Main Street on a sunny day, to visit the pharmacy for a necessity, or to stop in at the coffee shop for a drink. Every time I pass the brick building on the east side of the street, I read the sign: *For Sale, Artist's studio, 2nd floor*. I glance through the windowpanes set in the whitewashed wood and see a set of narrow gray stairs going straight up to a brown door. I wonder what's on the other side.

As my imagination churns with ideas, I walk through the entrance and up the gray stairs to the brown door at the top. I turn the knob slowly and push the door open. Inside, the floors are covered with clean white sheets. The walls are the same bright white. Colorful wooden frames hang on the walls, holding beautiful works of art. Easels bedeck the floor, holding canvases with unfinished paintings of bold, abstract shapes. Solid primary colors are splashed about the canvases and the entire room. Simple furniture rests around the perimeter of the studio: a blue armchair and a red chaise lounge with a yellow pillow. Windows let in light from two sides of the room, their sills supporting exotic-looking plants. In the middle of the ceiling hangs a spherical light with a red fixture...

I turn into the Mill Mountain Coffee Shop and order a strawberry flavored Italian Soda. I sit down at a small table near the back of the shop. As I sip the sweet red drink through a clear plastic straw, I observe my surroundings. Next to a large fireplace hangs a dark painting of a woman in black facing away from the viewer. This same painting hangs on the black wall of the artist's studio. Several similar paintings accent the shadowy walls. A deep purple carpet covers the entire floor, and an easel sits atop it on the right side of the room. Deep red curtains cover the single window. In the middle of the ceiling hangs a gothic chandelier...

I look down at my drink and see that only ice remains in the glass, so I rise from the table and leave the warm coffee shop. I bow my head as I face the cold December air on Main Street and I stuff my bare hands into the soft pockets of my fleece jacket. My hair flies wildly in the piercing wind, and my cheeks redden with the bitter cold. I turn onto North Broad Street and am suddenly faced with a great gust of the fierce wind blowing from the south. My eyes well up with icy tears and I duck through the white doorway, slamming it behind me. I stand in the cramped foyer between the outer door, with its For Sale sign showing backwards through the window, and those gray stairs going up to the studio.

The stairway is warm and I can hear the wind howling outside. I shiver just thinking about walking all the way back to school in that bitter air. I look up the stairs to the doorway. It seems a fine time to explore. Slowly, I creep up the dull gray stairs to the brown door. With butterflies in my stomach, I turn the knob and enter the studio.

Standing on the threshold, I see a hardwood floor covered in the center by a plush blue rug. On the opposite wall from me is a red brick fireplace with a blazing fire. The walls are a warm tawny color and hold a few wooden frames with paintings of birch trees and log cabins. In the far-right corner sits an easel and a mostly white canvas with the beginnings of a mountain scene painted on its upper edge. Blue curtains hang from the windows, matching the soft rug. In the middle of the ceiling hangs a soft light covered by a tawny shade...

The tears are streaming from my eyes, and my face and hands are numb with the bitter cold as I fumble for my keys to unlock the outer door of my residence hall. The night is getting late, so I climb the two flights of stairs, put on my pajamas and climb into bed. I rise up in the middle of the night with an intense feeling of curiosity. I grab a flashlight, pull a sweatshirt over my head and slide my feet into my sneakers. Under the starry sky, I walk swiftly to North Broad Street, breathing in the crisp night air. When I reach the white door and step into the stairwell, I turn on my flashlight to illuminate the gray steps. Creeping quietly, I follow the yellow beam to the brown door at the top of the stairs. When I reach it, I turn the handle and enter the room.

All around me, the studio is red. The floor is laid with solid red tile and the walls are painted in the same crimson shade. On the walls hang red frames with paintings of shapes in various hues of red. The window is covered by a heavy red shade. In the far-left corner is a red easel holding a solid red canvas. In the middle of the ceiling hangs a square-shaped red glass lampshade with a red light glowing behind it...

The sun kisses my face as it shines through the thin blinds in my dormitory window. I open my eyes, stretch, and get out of bed to dress. Feeling well rested, I spring down the stairs and knock on Bobby's door. He and I walk to the dining hall together for Saturday brunch. As we're eating scrambled eggs, biscuits, hash-browned potatoes, and apple juice, I tell him about the white door on North Broad Street. Being an adventurous person, he begs me to show him the entrance to the staircase so that he can see what lies behind the upper door. We clear our table and leave the Commons, heading straight for the artist's studio.

We make our way down the sidewalk opposite the empty Farmer's Market. I show Bobby the white door, and we go inside to the gray stairwell. My friend looks up at the brown door with curiosity in his eyes. My heart quickens with anticipation as we climb the stairs. At the top, Bobby turns the knob of the brown door and pushes it open. He reaches along the inner wall and feels around until he reaches the light switch. With a flip of his wrist, the studio is illuminated. We stand in the open doorway and look into the room.

The walls are off-white and bare, with the paint peeling off in places. The floor is unfinished, as the original linoleum or wood has been removed, and the entire surface is covered with a layer of white paint-dust. Near the far corner sits an empty red Coke can lying on its side, with a piece of used sandpaper a few feet away. The window is bare and one pane is slightly cracked. In the middle of the ceiling hangs a single light bulb...

About the author:

Jessica Hench, originally from Suffield, Connecticut is a student at Roanoke College in Salem, Virginia. She is an English major pursuing teaching certification. While this is her first short story, she has had several poems published and hopes to publish novels and children's stories in the future.

THE DEAD ZONE
©2000 by Craig Rondinone

BOBBY SUTTON HAD heard it all before. There was no word that could penetrate the armor of concentration that surrounded him. He fed off the venom of the fans whenever they went after him. It helped Bobby to do all he could to make sure his team was victorious, so every fan in attendance would go home angry and despondent. As he strolled to the plate, wiping the excess pine tar off his bat, the crowd began its verbal assault.

"Bobby, I met your momma by the batting cage! He's a real nice guy!"

"You're going home in a body bag!"

"Sutton sucks! Sutton sucks!"

"Johnson's going to make you his bitch, boy!"

The "Johnson" the fan was referring to was the pitcher, Jackie Johnson. His arsenal of pitches was limited. He was a fastball-curve guy. His fastball was average at best, but it looked faster when Johnson was getting his nasty curve over for strikes. Johnson had the reputation of throwing inside, sometimes at a batter's head if he looked too comfortable. He could be extremely intimidating.

Bobby wasn't intimidated, though. Not much scared him. Maybe his mother when he was nine and she whacked him with her shoe when he failed math. Maybe his pit bull when Bobby forgot to take him out before a doubleheader. Maybe his agent when he told Bobby there were only three teams willing to meet his ten million dollar a year asking price when he became a free agent. Not Johnson, though. Not any pitcher.

Bobby saw the pattern Johnson used on the first two batters of the inning and it seemed as if it would be similar for him. A steady diet of curves, with possibly a fastball snuck in to keep him honest. As Bobby dug in at the batter's box, the catcher started mouthing with him.

"Pop up on the first pitch," the catcher ordered as he beat his oversized mitt with his other hand. "My legs are getting tired down here."

"Pop one out of the park?" Bobby asked sarcastically. "Is that what you said? Well, flash your boy a sign to throw me something I can hit."

"Play ball!" the home plate umpire shouted. The battle was ready to begin. Bobby glared out at Johnson as if to silently say, "Bring it on!" Bobby took a few practice swings as Johnson shook off his catcher twice. Bobby knew this was a mind game since Johnson didn't have much to shake off. Bobby locked in mentally, almost hypnotically, on his foe. He began muttering to himself.

"Dead Zone. Dead Zone."

Bobby was talking about the area where the entire league knew not to throw the ball. "The Dead Zone" was anything low and inside that Bobby could turn on and pull down the right field line with his sweet left-handed swing. Fastball, curve, change-up, didn't matter. If you threw the ball in the zone, you and the ball were dead.

Bobby tried setting pitchers up by crowding the plate to force them to throw inside to back him off. If they made a mistake and instead of throwing at his head, missed a little lower, Bobby would make them pay ten times out of ten. Johnson was good for plenty of mistakes.

As Johnson wound up, Bobby guessed curve.

And, as he did about ten percent of the time, he guessed wrong.

Johnson threw a fastball, and he didn't miss. The pitch sailed out of his hand and right at Bobby's head. Bobby tried a last-ditch effort to turn away, but he was too far into his fooled swing to stop. The 88-mph pitch hit him flush in the face.

Bobby opened his eyes and couldn't believe he was not in pain. He saw the blue sky, the white clouds and the yellow sun hovering above him. As he lay on his back, motionless, he realized there was no sound. Nothing coming from the crowd. Nothing coming from either dugout. No trainer running on the field to help.

Silence.

Bobby sat up and looked around the stadium nervously. He was surrounded by empty seats in a barren ballpark. Everyone had gone home and left Bobby behind. It made no sense. Then Bobby noticed a rustling coming from the home team dugout. A man dressed in a black uniform decorated vertically with white stripes and the letter D embroidered over the heart walked out with a ball and glove. Bobby didn't recognize the uniform. He lifted himself off the ground and felt his face as the ballplayer dashed towards him. There were no marks on Bobby's face that weren't supposed to be there.

"Hello," the man said sternly as he reached Bobby, extending a hand to shake. "The name's Cross. I've always wanted to face you. I thought it would be a great challenge."

"What?" Bobby asked, dumbfounded, shaking cobwebs out of his head that weren't there. "What are you talking about?"

"Me versus you," Cross said as they shook. "*Mano a mano.* One on one. It's game time." Bobby still didn't know what Cross was babbling about. Cross went from being friendly to serious. "If you didn't know by now, you're on the verge of death."

"What?" Bobby screamed as he pulled his hand away. "What the hell—?"

"Don't say that word!" Cross exclaimed, putting his hand over Bobby's mouth before he could blurt out more. "Okay, here's the deal. That pitch you took in the face? It cracked your skull and bounced around your brains. You're teetering very gingerly on the thin line between life and death. The deal is you have to play your way back to living."

With that bit of information, Bobby used all his strength to push Cross's hand off. "There's no way this is happening!" he said as he took a step back. As he did, however, another stranger apprehended him. This guy was in the same uniform as Cross, only he was wearing catcher's gear. Bobby struggled as the man held his arms back.

Cross grew impatient. "If you want to have any chance of going back to being a living, breathing person, you better shut your mouth and listen!" Cross informed Bobby. Bobby complied. Cross took a deep breath and continued. "You're in a coma. You're lying in a hospital bed in an emergency room with a bunch of tubes and machines hooked up to you, and your family and friends are out in the waiting room, waiting for you to be wheeled into surgery. And don't think the Press isn't waiting there, too."

"Yeah, alright," Bobby whispered as the catcher let up on him, seeming to know Bobby was of no danger anymore. Another player in a black uniform ran into the outfield as Cross went on. "You get one at-bat. One chance. One time and one time only," Cross said as he pointed a single finger in Bobby's direction. "You have to hit a homerun off me. You hit a homer, you live. Anything less—single, double, triple, strikeout, groundout, flyout—you're dead."

"It's that simple?" Bobby asked.

"That simple."

"And if I refuse to do this?"

"Well," Cross said as he turned his back, "it'll go down in the boxscore as a forfeit, ergo a strikeout."

"Ergo my ass is in—"

"Uh, uh, uh," Cross reminded Bobby as he faced him. "Remember, not *that* word. And I didn't say where you'd be ending up once you died. That's not my decision. I just do the pitching. Joe does the catching, Phil does the fielding, and the guy with the big chest protector does the umpiring." With that, an umpire showed up behind the plate.

"Play ball!" he shouted to the four people in attendance. A bat appeared at Bobby's feet on the edge of the infield grass. It was like it was custom made. It was the weight and length Bobby liked. Even had the right amount of pine tar on the handle. The catcher squatted, the outfielder put his shades down as he positioned himself in center, and the umpire threw a ball to Cross as he stood on the pitching rubber.

"Why only one outfielder?" Bobby questioned as he dug in at the back of the box.

"That's all I need," Cross smugly replied as he felt up the ball. "He's insurance in case the ball comes close to the wall, but he's been rarely used over the decades." The catcher put down a sign, and Cross liked the choice. He reared back with an unorthodox right-handed motion Bobby hadn't seen before. Bobby couldn't pick up the release point, and Cross threw a perfect back-door slider on the outside corner.

"Strike one!" the umpire yelled with authority. Bobby wasn't worried. He was a solid hitter when behind in the count due to his short stroke. This wasn't any ordinary pitcher, though. "Nice pitch," Bobby said in a patronizing way. "I couldn't have hit it out of the park."

"It better be a good pitch," Cross said as he took another sign from his backstop. "I've been working on it for the last twenty-two years."

Bobby took a couple air swings, then focused in on his target. It was a picturesque day. It was cool, just like Bobby liked it. The lines were freshly painted. The grass was neatly cut. The infield dirt seemed hard and fast. Bobby liked the ballpark a lot. He started muttering to himself to get psyched up as Cross came set. "Dead Zone. Dead Zone."

Cross wound up and delivered. Bobby figured Cross could throw anything, especially ahead in the count. He guessed breaking ball, but as the ball came out of Cross's hand, Bobby didn't see a tight spin. He stopped from swinging early at what turned out to be a heater. The pitch was down the middle but a couple of inches below the knees.

"Strike two!"

"No way!" Bobby argued as he sneered at the ump. The outfielder laughed as the catcher tossed Cross the ball.

"Home field call, Bobby," Cross said with a sly grin. "You're not going to get the close calls here. This is my house! You better be swinging."

Bobby didn't like his odds now. This game was no longer fun. Down 0-2 to a pitcher he had never seen before, in the battle of his life, *for* his life, was not what he had in mind. Bobby had never felt like this. Helpless. Powerless. Intimidated.

Cross got another sign he liked. It was like his catcher was on the same wavelength. Bobby talked to himself again, but this time it was like he was praying. "Dead Zone. Dead Zone." Cross showed him another look, another arm angle, another release point. He went sidearm after going over the top the first two pitches. The pitch sailed towards Bobby's head, which was out over the plate since Bobby was looking outside corner. He ducked at the last instant to escape another beaning.

"Ball one!"

Even the most biased umpire couldn't call that pitch a strike. Bobby was on the seat of his pants staring out at Cross. He picked himself up and dusted off, but he never took his eyes off Cross.

"Don't think I didn't have a scouting report on you," Cross told Bobby. "I know what you like to do up there."

Bobby was now more determined than ever. He was sick and tired of Cross's act. He wanted to live. He'd do anything he could to make it a reality.

Where would Cross go now? Would he stay outside, away from Bobby's strength, since he knew how dangerous Bobby was with inside pitches? Or was he cocky enough, and talented enough, to actually come inside, thinking Bobby wasn't looking for it? Bobby wasn't so sure until Cross did something he hadn't done yet: he shook off his catcher. Maybe there was trouble in paradise?

"Dead Zone. Dead Zone."

Cross went with a higher leg kick and came with a three-quarters delivery. Bobby had seen three pitches, and now he could pick up the release and the ball, no problem. Bobby's 20/20 vision let him see the pointer and middle fingers spread out on the seems. The ball came out as a fastball, but Bobby knew better. It was a splitter. It dropped off the table halfway to the plate. It had great movement. It was a perfect pitch—to hit.

"Thank you," Bobby said as he hacked. The sound of the violence between ball and bat was deafening. The ball flew like a bullet down the right field line. It curved towards the foul pole, but nobody took any chances. The outfielder ran full speed from straight-away center to the line as soon as the ball left the bat. Cross beat his fist into his glove, appearing to know he'd underestimated Bobby's talent. Bobby ran like the wind to first base. He wasn't about to be caught up in a technicality. Cross said Bobby needed a home run, but he didn't say the homer had to be out of the park. An inside-the-park homer would do just as well.

The ball crashed against the right field wall with a sickening thud. "Fair ball!" the umpire screamed, seemingly unhappy with the outcome. Bobby ran around second base like Death was chasing him. Bobby had above-average speed, and he knew there was no stop sign waiting for him at third base. He had to go the route.

The outfielder tracked down the ball as Bobby was halfway to third. He juggled the ball, then had trouble getting it out of his glove. Finally, as Bobby was rounding third widely and heading for home, the fielder threw a rocket at the catcher. The catcher's mask was off and he was blocking the plate. Bobby wasn't used to having to sacrifice his body, but he had to make an exception in this case. In between third and home, Bobby saw the ball bounce to the side of the pitcher's mound and skid to the catcher. Bobby lowered his shoulder and hit the catcher the exact moment the ball did.

The collision was monstrous. The echo of a bone cracking would have made the normal mortal vomit. Luckily, it wasn't Bobby's bone. The catcher, his collarbone broken on impact, was lying prone and in severe pain on his back. Bobby was on top of him, belly to belly with his opponent. The catcher cared about only one thing, and it wasn't preventing Bobby from scoring. As the catcher clutched his injured area, Bobby tried to take advantage. Bobby pried the catcher's mitt open. There was no ball inside the pocket.

Bobby was a mere five feet away from his ticket to staying alive, home plate. He shook the cobwebs out of his head and then dragged himself off the catcher. The collision sapped most of the energy out of his body, but there was a slight reserve left in the tank. On his hands and knees, Bobby crawled towards the dirt-stained plate. His pace was slow but sure. Bobby blocked everything out of his mind, concentrating fully on reaching his glorious destination. He didn't know where the ball was. He didn't care.

Ten seconds felt like ten hours. A minute felt like an eternity. Bobby's tired and battered muscles wouldn't allow him to end the agony quicker. He scratched and clawed to the point where he was one arm-length away from home, but before he could stretch for it, he felt something gently touch him on his back.

"You're out!"

Bobby stopped in his tracks. He knew what had happened. He let his body collapse in a heap on the warm dirt. He was a defeated man.

"Fundamentals," Cross said with a sly grin. He hovered over Bobby like the sun. He left his glove, with the ball inside it, on Bobby's back. "The pitcher always has to back up on a play at the plate."

The afternoon was cool and comfortable. The sun didn't overpower the ballpark with steamy rays. The lines were as white as the driven snow. The infield was playing fast and furious. The dirt was nice and hard, and the grass was chopped to where it looked like artificial turf. The sky was cloudless. It was a perfect day to play an important baseball game.

Bobby strode to the plate like a man on a mission. He slapped his bat on his heels to loosen the dirt from his cleats. As he stepped into the batter's box, he looked back at the catcher and shared some playful banter.

"Pop one out on the first pitch," the catcher told Bobby as he smashed his knuckles in the pit of his mitt.

"I'll wait until I get my pitch, thank you," Bobby replied. He took a couple of practice swings and felt real good. "Maybe I'll rope it down the line and make it interesting."

The pitcher on the neatly groomed mound was albino-pale. His name was Mitchell, and this was the biggest pressure situation he'd ever been in. Bobby watched him as he swung a couple more times. Mitchell had spots forming under his arms because he was sweating so profusely. The poor guy was shaking since he was so nervous. Bobby wanted to feel sorry for him, but his head took control of his heart. It was time to go to work.

"Play ball!" the umpire instructed.

Cross sat quietly in the dugout with a clipboard in hand. He was ready to jot down some notes for a scouting report. He liked to chart the pitches for future reference. Cross didn't have too humongous of an ego to think there would never be a pitcher to come around with better stuff than he had. In fact, Cross *wanted* Mitchell on his team. He began cheering for Bobby under his breath.

Mitchell looked in for a sign and he agreed with the first one he saw. This just made clear to Bobby what he thought all along: Mitchell was throwing a first-pitch fastball to get ahead in the count.

"Dead Zone. Dead Zone."

As Bobby did ninety percent of the time, he guessed right.

Fastball.

Dead Zone.

New teammate.

About the Author:

Craig Rondinone is a syndicated fantasy sports columnist for SportsTicker, a sports news service located in Jersey City, New Jersey. His weekly columns have appeared on web sites for ESPN, Sporting News, Yahoo and Excite. His newest book, Ten Tales to make your head explode (PublishAmerica) was published in 2004. Craig lives in Brick, New Jersey and enjoys the finer things in life— pro wrestling, soft tacos and deep thinking.

THE LAST COOL SUMMER
©2001 by Vincent Guiliano

BREEZES WERE HARD to come by during the hot summer days in Fairview. Jeffrey and I would rush to Stoaks Deli and pretend to be looking in the cooler as we struggled to point our faces into the cold damp air. Mr. Stoaks was always angry, especially when kids hung around the store without buying anything. Hearing him getting closer, we fought for one last cool breeze flowing among the cans of Brown Cow and tall orange Nehi soda bottles. "Hey! Let's go there, boys, buy something or get out!" Once again surrounded by unbearable heat, we'd stroll along The Avenue, punching each other's arms and stopping only to burst the bubbles of hot water seeping up from the softening asphalt along The Avenue. "Even the street is sweating," Jeffrey would say.

Summers in Fairview were as magical to me as they were sad. Jeffrey was my only friend, and he always threatened to go to his air-conditioned house if I didn't do what he wanted. It was during these summers that I learned of my intolerance for the heat and for anyone getting the better of me. I would call his bluff and end up spending most of my time finding shade and wishing the sun would go down and leave me in the relative peace of still, steamy, New Jersey night air. Solitude, I learned, was not so bad. I would pace our apartment trying to find cool spots on the walls to lean against and splash cool water on my face, a momentary relief, made slightly better by fanning myself with the top of an old shoebox. My father was entitled to the only electric fan in our apartment because, as my mother would say, "He needs to sleep so

95

he can go to work." At 11 years old, you were not that important.

I must have memorized every design in the painted steel ceiling of my bedroom. Lying awake, I'd move from side to side in my bed trying not to stay on the hot spot too long. Fireflies drifted past the window screens and the constant din of insects filled the room as I struggled to sleep, thinking about tomorrow.

In the early afternoon, I would ask my mother for money and take the 22 Hillside bus down The Avenue to the Embassy Theater in the next town. The hot, bumpy ride was worth it. I would pull the cord and jump off when it stopped at the corner, running straight to the box office. The banner over the door read "Cooled by Refrigeration" with a picture of a smiling white bear sitting on a melting ice cube. "Lucky bear," I thought as I slipped the coins under the rusty iron bars and held the precious ticket in my sweaty hands.

The first gust of cool air was so hypnotically fulfilling, I would stand still and stare at the crystal chandeliers in the lobby, losing myself in their glow. Inside, I'd sit on plush red velvet seats with warm popcorn and candy bars in my lap, sinking into the cold darkness of the theater, wondering why the floor was so sticky and waiting for the Double Feature to begin. It was a day in heaven at eighty cents a pop.

One hazy June morning of the following year, I again braced for the long hot summer that lay ahead, and wandered alone through the neighborhood, delirious from the oppressive heat, yet determined to keep my head in Stoaks' cooler until the neon clock approached matinee time. Soon ejected from the store yet again, I found comfort in knowing that I stole some extra cooler time. Jeffrey would have been proud. Even at the mercy of the cruel mid-day sun, I summoned new vigor borne amid fantasies of the refuge I would soon reach and ran home to get the precious money necessary to buy it.

I jumped off the bus and ran through toward the theater, but something was different this time. The Embassy Theater was closed. Thick wooden boards were nailed over the box office windows and a long silver chain looped through the old brass door handles, joined together by a rusty padlock. The banner was still up and the bear was still chilling on the cube.

The bus ride back home was the worst, knowing I would have to face the rest of this summer without my sanctuary. The private heaven I loved was gone for good and all that is left now are the memories of gladiator movies, buttered popcorn and those hot summer afternoons spent hiding in the dark, cool abyss of the theater.

About the author:

Vincent Guiliano was born and raised in Fairview, NJ and attended Rutgers University where he graduated in 1975 with a BA in Psychology and a minor in creative writing. He now lives with his family in Southern California.

SWIMMING TOWARD THE BUTTERSCOTCH MAN

©2000 by Elizabeth Benton Appell

ON THE DAY he was hired at a cutting-edge technology company at a salary more than four times what I make as a librarian, we went together to the Harley-Davidson dealership. It was a windy autumn in San Francisco and a heightened clarity existed in the air. Everything snapped with electricity including the pocked-face salesman when he touched one of the massive shiny machines. After a rancorous negotiation, we rode into the cold on a FLHRC Road King Classic with AM/FM stereo, CB radio, cruise control and a rubber mounted 1450cc Twin Cam 88 engine. Putting my arms around Lawrence's waist (I called him Law), a current shot between us and we roared like bandits down the Great Highway that snaked the Pacific Ocean. Flecks of grit ticked against our helmets and dry air raced coarsely past my face, drawing tears from my eyes. When he geared down and the bike thrust forward, I felt as though we would live forever.

We rode until the sun singed the horizon and then exhausted, we went to my place. Evening pressed against the windows of my Russian Hill flat and soon faded from pewter to black as I scrambled eggs, sliced crusty sourdough, and poured glasses of Chardonnay. For the first time since we'd met two years ago at a microbrewery, he said, "I love you, Lily."

I was stunned. Law was truly beautiful, tall and broad shouldered. His cheeks flushed in a way that made him look new and innocent though the butterscotch skin surrounding his hopeful eyes faintly creased with the promise of his oncoming forties. Freckles sprinkled like tiny islands across his cheeks. Most of the women I know would trade a free checking account at Saks for this man's attention. I wasn't worthy. I'm plain.

"Don't say that," I said. "Don't talk about love. You'll spoil what we have."

Since the beginning we referred to ourselves as the Gemini. On weekends we bashed through rave concerts and rented Jane Austin movies using the remote to stop the tape when we wanted to parody a scene. On weeknights he'd call me from his condo for which he'd paid all cash, and we'd talk on the telephone until the public television station went off the air and the screen turned to snow.

"Love is the precursor to friendship," he said. I had been under the illusion that it was the other way around. I'd not allowed us to become sexual and he surprisingly had gone along. Only twice had he pushed.

"Lil, please." He had drawn me toward him and I'd made a gun out of my hand and stuck the barrel up his nose. Another time we did kiss, but I bit his lip. His blood tasted like burned bacon and he didn't go to work the next day. Once he sucked my fingers and asked, "What are you afraid of?"

"After sex comes disappointment, bitterness, and anger," I said.

"Now there's an upbeat, optimistic view," he said and took my shoulders in his big butterscotch hands and drew me near. His breath was sweet like summer hay and his blue eyes icy. I wanted to kiss him, to fall into him, but always I'd pull back. Nobody really loves, do they?

"I've never seen love work," I whispered.

"That's rich," he said rearing back, filling the room with his deep cracking laugh. "Don't you see how we are together and how sweet it is?"

We went to more movies and concerts and he always paid because he was the one making six figures, and afterward at small restaurants we'd argue politics. "God damn righteous Republicans," he said and his hand would come down on the table causing every glass to jump and drops of wine to land on the white linen where they bloomed like small red roses. "Do you know if it weren't for big government there'd still be slavery?"

"What a treat to be a slave," I said. "No options."

"Marry me, Lil."

"Sorry," was my answer and the blue in his eyes faded and his butterscotch skin paled. I think first he was angry and then disappointed, because he left the restaurant, his head bowed. He didn't look back. I paid that bill.

We didn't talk for weeks. Finally, I called him and we made a date for dinner. I arrived first at The Stinking Rose and ordered a bottle of Chianti. He was late. Three glasses of wine later he still hadn't shown up. Maybe he'd changed his mind, I thought, because he just doesn't think I'm worth it. When I heard his Harley roar up outside, something leaped inside me. He stomped across the restaurant, shrugged off his black leather jacket, and sat down. I shocked myself when I leaned forward and said, "I never want to be without you."

"Then why won't you—"

I put my hand over his mouth. "Because if we keep things the way they are, we'll never hurt each other."

His big hand came down harder than ever before and this time rivers of wine veined over the white cloth. "You've already hurt me!"

He was right. And then he whispered, "I could never hurt you."

"You couldn't help it. It's what people do," I said.

"Well," he said. "That's that." He laid money on the table and ironed it with his hand. "I want more. I'm sorry, but I want more. Good luck, Lil. I hope the cage you're building is to your liking, because you're going to live in it alone for a very long time."

I watched him walk away. His shoulders hunched, his jacket slung over one arm. I listened to the roar of the motorcycle until I couldn't hear it anymore.

He's right, I thought. The recognition caused panic to boil up like vomit and squeeze into every corner of my spare childhood, washing over the memories of a drunken father bellowing at a drunken mother, "You're a sot, a flabby sodden sot and I don't care if you know. I love someone else!" Fear swamped me like an angry ocean pummeling a small boat. I was sinking and couldn't breathe.

I stumbled out of the restaurant onto the street where a dirty batting of clouds hung low. I caught a bus and rocked home.

When I entered the flat, the telephone was ringing. Please be Law, I said out loud. Crossing the room, I noted the bare floors, the bare windows, pale art on my walls. Everything colorless and lonely. I love you, Law, I said and picked up the phone.

—Law? (Hesitation.)

—Yes, I'm Lawrence's friend.

—Of course, I'll come. Which hospital?

And then the voice buzzed details through the telephone using impossible words such as skid, ignited, totaled. Terrible attributions I had difficulty understanding.

In the taxi I fingered a St. Christopher's medal. I don't know where it had come from. Maybe the bottom of my purse which, though used daily, hadn't been emptied, let alone explored, for at least two years. I ran my fingers over the smooth silver medal with the sweet smiling saint in the center and it felt satisfying and orderly and assured me that everything was about to fall into place.

But when I stood outside Law's hospital room, I knew that whatever order had existed in my life had been taken away.

A doctor with tired eyes told me that when Law had left the restaurant, his Harley had hit an oil slick on Bay Street and careened into a car and his bike had exploded. His spinal cord at the thoracic level had been crushed, which meant he probably would never walk again.

The nursing staff required me to scrub before I entered his room and someone helped me into a gown and a mask. At the doorway one of the nurses instructed me not to touch him and then mumbled something about I shouldn't be shocked when I see him.

I hurried toward the silent figure in bed, but stopped when I saw him connected to tubes and a mechanical sighing lung. I swallowed a silent gasp. They hadn't told me about the burns.

His face, his neck and shoulders: he looked like a candle that had been burning through an entire dinner party.

He opened his eyes and looked at me. They were still blue and the only thing about him that hadn't changed.

"Law," I gulped. I stood for a long time looking at him. Though he made a futile attempt to raise a butterscotch hand, I swam like crazy in my ocean of fear.

And then a glisten of tears welled in his eyes.

"Law," I whispered and began stroking with all the force I could muster. Shore was in sight. "Law, I . . .I . . .I'll marry you. I *will* marry you!"

A muffled grunt came from deep inside the candle. "I'm ugly. And helpless."

"No," I whispered, "You're different." I felt my feet touch ground. I'd made the crossing. "That's all. You're just different."

About the author:

Elizabeth writes screenplays, plays and novels as well as short stories. Her first play, "Confessions of a Catholic Child" was a finalist in the Writer's Network Fiction Contest in Los Angeles, chosen for staged reading by The Long Beach Playhouse, finished fifth in a field of 9,000 in the 1998 Writer's Digest Playwriting Competition, and optioned by a Canadian producer to create a one-hour film based on the play. Her second play, "Moon Walkers" finished second out of a field of 300 in the Do Gooder Productions New Playwright Award Competition, was recognized as a semi-finalist in Writer's Network 1998 competition, was part of New Theatre Works Festival 99 in Santa Rosa, became a semi-finalist in the Writer's Network Screenplay & Fiction Competition and placed in the top ten plays out of a field of 19,000 in the

October 2000 Writer's Digest Writing Competition. Her "Journal of a Common Man," won Dominican University's Festival of Short Plays. Elizabeth recently completed her fourth novel, "Lessons from the Gypsy Camp" (published by Scribes Valley Publishing, March 2004).

NURSERY LAND BLUES
©2000 by Husein Taherbhai

THE HUGE, two-block long Victoria Railway Terminal at Bori Bunder stood as a testimony to the splendor of Victorian architecture. Today, as on every day of the year, it was teeming with crowds of Indians on their daily commute within the city of Mumbai. However, the majestic exterior beauty of the regal structure was in sharp contrast with the interior, which reeked of the stench of unclean urinals and masses of humanity. The queue for purchasing tickets for the commute was long but it moved intermittently with surprising efficiency provided by the world's largest railway network.

The monsoons had long set in. Today, the rains were extremely heavy, and the wind howled and blew with a force that turned umbrellas upside down. Occasionally, people stopped in mid-street, turning sideways in their futile attempt at countering the full-frontal blast of a fresh, unbalancing onslaught of Mother Nature's fury. Those women who were foolish enough to wear skirts had, on occasion, been embarrassed when the mighty wind had caught them off-guard and exposed their wet underwear. Not even the affluent Indians with their London Fog raincoats could keep themselves from being soaked.

The torrential rainwater could not find an escape through Mumbai's inadequate drainage system. It was rising fast, hiding dangerously submerged potholes that were known to have dire consequences on some of the less fortunate commuters. There were puddles inside the station, too, created by dripping, rain-soaked people who hastily entered the station, shaking their plastic wrappings, raincoats, and umbrellas as they hurried towards the crowded trains or waited impatiently at the ticket counter.

Not all people who entered the sparsely lit terminal, however, were travelers. There were the usual shop owners who sold newspapers, magazines, candy, food, and baggage. There were also those who worked for the Indian Railway, their over-used, faded uniforms a sure sign of government employees earning government wages. Then there were those who had no place to go. They too had a business, but their business of begging had no legitimate standing. These ragamuffins' existence was considered a hindrance by those who worked or passed through the station which in turn provoked a constant effort by the municipality to drive the beggars beyond the boundaries of the sprawling city.

A little girl stood in the shadows cast by the giant arches of the Victoria Terminal. It was stiflingly hot and humid inside the station, but Kanchan was used to the vagaries of the weather. She had no covering to keep the rains away from her malnourished, pot-bellied body, and the torn, dirty dress, hanging loosely on her tiny frame, provided little comfort from the ravages of the climate. Today, however, she had not ventured out of the building except when she had to relieve herself on the railway tracks in the early hours of the morning. She stood with a few *paisas* in her begging bowl wondering if it was time to approach her mother, Geetabai, for food.

So far, the crowd had not been too receptive to her cries for alms. She and her brother had been well trained by their mother, and they knew, after some years of practice, who to approach and what type of plea to use to obtain the best response. Today, however, the crowd seemed to be in a weather-induced, nasty mood, and there were not many among them with charitable hearts. With only a few *paisas* in her bowl, Kanchan knew there was not enough money to buy food. She was afraid to ask her mother for something to eat because she knew her mother would scold her for her extremely poor productivity. Perhaps her stepbrother, Ramu, was having better luck. He was working the crowds on the other side of the large building.

"What are you staring at me for, child?" Geetabai asked.

"Nothing. We don't have much money today. I have only managed to collect a few *paisas* and it is already late in the morning."

"Well? What do you want me to do? Ah. Ah . . .h, ah," Geetabai started coughing as she lay curled up, shivering on the cold hard floor of the railway station. "Perhaps things will improve when the tourists come out in the evening—if the rains end by then." Geetabai knew that most tourists did not frequent Mumbai at this time of the year. The few that did, generally ventured forth from their hotels only when the rains stopped and the morning sun slowly advanced to the outstretched arms of the horizon—at a time when it was relatively cooler from the stifling monsoon heat.

"Ma, I am hungry," Kanchan finally picked up her courage.

"What can I give you? I don't have anything. Since you don't have money to buy food, go see if you can find something in that restaurant's garbage dump."

As if on cue, Ramu joined them. He was almost an inch shorter than his younger sister. His nose was running, and there was an open-sore on his arm that seemed badly infected. "Nobody is giving anything today," he said, shaking his empty bowl. "I only have one *rupee*. Not enough to buy even a single *batata vada*."

Geetabai coughed, unable to rid herself of the chest cold that had persisted for almost a month now. Her body burned and it seemed that she lost her temper more often with the kids now that she was sick.

"Do I have to teach you two all over again how to beg? Can't you do anything right? Go on, you useless children, go find something from that restaurant's garbage dump. I will heat up whatever you bring and make something hot for us," she visibly shivered and wrapped her flimsy *sari* a little tighter around her body. She had no blouse and the occasional draft of hot breeze felt very cold on her burning bare arms and desiccated breasts. "Go on. Get out of my sight," she scolded them again. "Get something before we all have to go another day without food."

"Come on, Ramu, let's go." Kanchan put her dirt-caked arms around her seven-year-old brother and led him towards the garbage dump. The savory aroma of fried food assailed them but they curbed their yearning and headed for the narrow alley behind the restaurant. Perhaps, they would, like their mother had said, get lucky with the foreigners in the evening. If only the rains would stop.

It was almost four-thirty p.m. when the two rain-drenched children returned to their mother.

"Ma, look what I found!" said Kanchan excitedly. She pulled out a long, four-foot by two-foot, relatively dry piece of rectangular cloth and dangled it in front of her mother. The white piece of cloth was soiled brown with dirt and smelled equally bad, but it was no worse than the clothes the three of them had on. Geetabai looked at the cloth carefully.

"Good," she said gratefully and wrapped it carefully around the top part of her body. Then, seeing Ramu without a shirt, her maternal instinct rose in spite of her feverish condition. She unwrapped herself slowly and handed the cloth to her son.

"Ah. Ah...h, ah," she coughed. "You go ahead—keep it. I don't need it," she lied. "Take care of it or somebody will steal it from you. Ah, ah..." She once again went into a coughing fit.

"Ma, I have something, too," said Ramu. "Here, I found a whole package of half-eaten *bhel puri*. I know we cannot heat it but we also have this rice and I found this piece of half-eaten chicken that you can put in the water for soup. There is still some meat on the bone."

"Bless you children," Geetabai said feebly. "I don't want anything. I am not feeling too good. Why don't you two heat up the water and put this piece of bone and the rice in it? We don't have any salt but I have some *haldi* (turmeric) and *thana* (cumin) wrapped in that paper over there. Ah. Ah. Ah . . ." Geetabai started coughing. "Go on now, start the fire," she said as soon as her coughing subsided.

The two children went to a pile of papers and wooden sticks that their mother kept for the fire. They knew they were taking a chance at building a fire inside the building. The one-man security would come down on them real fast, but perhaps he would not notice their activity today. Ramu had seen him loitering on the other side of the huge, over-crowded building. Besides, there was no way they could go out on the sidewalk and cook their meal in the rain.

"Ma, where are the matches? I can't find them," Kanchan shouted.

The mother turned around and mumbled something that the children did not understand. Kanchan went up to her to get a response at a closer range.

"I don't know. Perhaps we are out of them," Geetabai murmured.

"Ma says we don't have any matches," Kanchan shouted at Ramu.

"I guess we will have to eat the rice without heating it," said Ramu, reluctantly. "I will wrap the bone in the paper. We may be able to use it when Ma feels a little better tomorrow."

The two children ravenously attacked their meager fare. "Ma, do you want some?" Ramu walked over to his mother. Geetabai made an incomprehensible sound and went back to sleep.

The next day proved to be just as stifling as the day before, but luckily it had stopped raining. At around eleven, the two children had collected five *rupees* (about 10 cents) between them. They were anxiously waiting for the *Chaiwalla* (tea seller) to arrive. If only they had one more *rupee*, they could have bought one cup of *chai* for each of them. Ramu was the first to spy the *Chaiwalla*, but before he could relay the message to his sister, they heard the car sirens in the distance that signaled the arrival of the police. Every month or two, the beggars were beaten out of the building by the city police or carried to the slum area far from the Terminal. The beggars, however, immediately returned after the departure of the police or, at the most, in a day or two when the politicians had lost interest in them.

"It is bad for our city's image," the Mayor of Mumbai had often declared in an effort at revitalizing his constituency's commitment for a vote on his seat in the next elections. "We will do everything in our power to eradicate the beggars from our public places," he had shouted. In turn, the city had responded with claps and chanting of, "Get rid of those polluters! They hurt business and are an eye-sore for our wonderful city!"

At the first sound of the sirens, Kanchan hastily picked up their meager belongings, ready to run. There was nothing much to carry except their three begging bowls, a rudiment of what was considered to be their spices, and the papers and sticks they used for building a fire. The children were used to this ritual occurrence. However, this time, their mother was not in the forefront guiding them to safety. On the contrary, she just moaned and lay shivering on the black, smooth stone floor, uncaring about the commotion around her. Ramu pulled at his mother's arms with all his might but only managed to turn her around. The scrawny woman was too heavy for his thin, little body.

The two children watched in horror as policemen, wielding long, thick sticks called *lathis*, descended upon the homeless beggars that had taken shelter under the roof of the Victoria Terminal.

"Ma, please, they will beat us and take us far away to the slums if you don't move!" the children cried.

At the last minute, under the strength of some hidden reserve, the wild-eyed Geetabai finally acknowledged the commotion around them. She saw the mass exodus of the beggars from the building. Comprehension of their predicament finally seeped its way to her feverish brain. Her terror at the sight of the *lathi*-swinging policemen ignited one last ounce of resolve at maintaining an appropriate distance from them. She barely managed to raise herself up, but with the help of her two scared children, she dragged her sick, feverish body from the building, out into the street. Her efforts further aggravated her pitiful condition and she soon collapsed on the sidewalk. Fortunately, she had progressed enough to be out of range of the policemen.

"We did it! Ma, we did it!" the two children shouted in innocent glee.

"Ok, leave me alone, children," she murmured.

As soon as the policemen had departed, the children bought two cups of piping hot *chai*, emptied about two-thirds in their begging bowls and the rest in their mother's bowl. They sipped their tea slowly, savoring the extra-sugar, milk-laden, piping-hot brew.

As they contentedly sat on the wooden bench outside the Terminal, sipping their *chai*, Ramu noticed the feared slumlord, Rakeshbhai, gliding towards them on his sleek bicycle.

"How are you kids doing?" he asked, feigning concern. He rode the bicycle right on top of the sidewalk and screeched to a stop in front of them.

"Fine," Kanchan replied as Ramu bravely placed himself between his sister and Rakeshbhai, who sat perched on his tilted bicycle with one leg firmly planted on the ground.

"We do not have to talk to you," Ramu said with defiance.

"Why? What have I done to you? Here, I mean no harm," Rakeshbhai said, reaching in his pocket for a couple of sweets. "Go on take it," he urged.

Kanchan extended her hand to receive the delicacy but Ramu snatched her hand back. "Don't you remember what Ma has told us?" he admonished his sister.

"Come on, stop kidding yourselves, children. You know your Ma is dying. Who will you go to when she dies, uh? Now, if you are nice to me, I will be more than willing to help you."

"Our mother is not dying," said both children in unison. Kanchan started crying.

"Please leave us alone," said Ramu. "We know you take children and cut off their arms or legs so people will be more inclined to give them alms. Our mother has told us everything, and so has one-armed Rahim who used to beg in that corner over there. Rahim told us he worked for you and you had cut-off one of his arms when he was very young. Where is he now? What has happened to him?"

"He, like you, used to talk too much, little boy. I believe he had an accident. That's what happens to children who talk too much. Anyway, by the looks of *your* arm, you will have to amputate it, too. If you don't, it will poison your whole body, and you will die in the gutters, just like your mother over there. Remember, amputating an arm or a leg can be very, very painful. But I can have it done through a certified doctor. He will give you the right medicine and put you to sleep before he touches you. I promise you, you will not feel a thing. I don't have much time now, but think of what I am saying. It is for your own good. Your mother will not last for more than a day or two. If you want, I can arrange a decent cremation for her. She would appreciate that, wouldn't you agree?"

"Leave us alone!" Ramu shouted defiantly. "We don't want anything to do with you." Then, taking his sister's arm he led her away from Rakeshbhai towards their mother.

The *chai* was still reasonably warm, and they took it over to Geetabai with anticipation of a rise in her flagging spirit. Their mother, however, did not show any interest in a brew that she usually cherished so much. She just lay on the sidewalk in a half-comatose state.

"I am going to help you, Ma," Kanchan said as she tried to raise her mother while Ramu brought the tin bowl close to her mouth.

"Drink up, Ma," Ramu said.

Geetabai took a sip, hoping that it would relieve her of the pain, but her bowels churned and she threw up, her empty stomach heaving with unbearable pain. She groaned loudly. Kanchan cradled her mother's head in her lap and cleaned her with the cloth that Ramu unwrapped from around his chest. Together, the two children managed to drag their mother a short distance away from her "throw-up." Ramu then took the cloth to a puddle in the street and washed it, failing to see the blood that was interspersed with the remnants of a few grains of rice in his mother's vomit.

Two days passed. The children's mother no longer grunted or coughed. She just lay there quietly while the children felt joy in the hope that their mother was finally getting better. She had never let them down and, except for the last few days when she had been too sick, she had always been there for them when they needed her.

"Please sir, will you help, us? Can you spare a *rupee*?" Both the children's begging bowls seemed fuller today than they had been in quite some time. Perhaps it was because the sun had finally come out from behind the clouds that the masses were in such a charitable mood. Standing at the entrances to the building, the children had already amassed forty *rupees* between them. Ma surely will be pleased with us today, they thought. It was getting dark but, surprisingly, a bus drove up with tourists and the children curbed their urges to buy food and go back to their mother.

"Please, madam, just one *rupee*. God will bless you and fill your coffers with untold wealth," they continued begging in the hope of breaking their mother's all-time collection record set during last year's *Diwali* festival.

It was late in the evening as the two starving children walked towards their mother. She still lay on the sidewalk just outside the Victoria Terminal. The children had not managed to bring her back into the building after the policemen had charged at them with their *lathis*. As they approached their mother, they broke into a run, anxious to show-off their collection for the day.

As they came within sight of Geetabai, they were somewhat awed by the flies that buzzed around their mother's body. In the rainy season, the filthy flies were a constant harassment to their living condition but, tonight, it seemed that the corner where their mother lay swarmed with an unusually large number of the grossly fat, purple-bellied insects. They were crawling all over their mother and she was doing nothing to dissuade them from entering the crevices of her nose, her open eyes, and her mouth. Knowing instinctively that something was wrong, they wailed for her response to their greeting, but were only met by silence. It was not long before they both started crying.

"Ma, please get up! Please say something! You are so cold. Here, you can have my piece of cloth. I promise I will find another one for you—a big, thick piece of cloth to give you extra warmth. Please get up!" Ramu tugged at the lifeless body.

"Ma, I will be very good. Look at the amount of money we have collected! We can buy lots of hot food today. Please wake up, Ma. Wake up. I will never bother you again if you just wake up!" cried Kanchan.

In the shadows, not far from Geetabai, Rakeshbhai watched the two children struggling with their mother's lifeless body. "She got what she deserved," he exclaimed. "How dare that beggar-woman spurn my advances when I asked her to stay with me?" he demanded of his *chamcha* (stooge), who doubled both as his ego-builder and as an accomplice in his sinister plots. "And how dare she call it a rape when she made only token gestures in repelling my advances? Any real man would have done the same, don't you agree?" he rhetorically asked his *chamcha*, who eagerly nodded his approval at his master's reasoning. "She should have been grateful for my attention. This would not have happened to her if she had. The ungrateful wretch could not even take care of the children. Perhaps she will be eternally grateful now that I am going to spread my protective umbrella over her precious children," he sneered.

Rakeshbhai looked with disgust at Geetabai's infected body. The municipality would send someone to clear the corpse when enough people complained about the stink. He had done his part and had already called them to clear the streets of the disease-ridden corpse. He had also asked his *chamcha* to complain to the municipality about the rotting cadaver and the other filth spread on their streets. The slumlord knew that by now others would have complained, too. He was sure that the municipality would be there no later than early tomorrow morning.

Rakeshbhai was sure that his son, Ramu, would quickly get used to the loss of a limb if food filled his belly on a regular basis. Actually, if it had not been for Ramu's infectious arm, he would just as well have drugged him into a stupor everyday instead of spending money on amputation–drugs, after all, were so much cheaper than a doctor's visit. Besides, a convulsing little boy, foaming from his mouth evoked the same, if not more, sympathy from those pretentious do-gooders as did a limbless boy. As for Kanchan, he had other plans for her. In a few years, she would be old enough to provide him with siblings that would assure him a continued supply of good income. He knew that it was only a matter of time before the two children would succumb to his demands. "Where else could they go?" Rakeshbhai consoled himself. A little force would have to be used, as a last resort, if those foolish children did not agree to his wishes. However, he wished that it would not come to that. Using force was so unbecoming of him.

About the author:

Husein Taherbhai was born in Bahrain and lived his childhood years in India. He has traveled to many different parts of the world and is currently working as a Psychometrician with The Psychological Corporation: Harcourt Educational Measurement. Husein received his doctorate from the University of South Florida and has been published in various scientific journals. He has also presented several papers at the National Council of Measurement in Education. In his spare time, Husein relaxes by painting in mix-media, and writing short stories and poems. Currently he is intermittently writing a screen play which he hopes to complete by the end of 2003.

THE MEANING OF MEAT
©2000 by Liz Morrison

IF YOU CRAWL underneath the picnic table in the backyard of my Aunt Rivka and Uncle Herb's house, you'll find my initials carved in the underside of the table. I don't think anyone else knows they're there. I was twelve and it was the first of many times I would hear Aunt Rivka tell the story of how she and Uncle Herb met Marilyn Monroe in Niagara Falls in 1955. The story must have lulled me into an artistic trance because next to my initials I carved three flowers and the words *Flower Power*.

Sitting at the picnic table with Aunt Rivka and my mother, I reach underneath to feel my roughly carved artwork from a few years back.

"Ruthie, did I ever tell you about the first time your Uncle Herb and I went to Niagara Falls? We were on our honeymoon and we ran right into Marilyn Monroe, right there on the street. She was walking along just like a regular person. I even had my picture taken with her." I didn't want to listen to this story again.

"I need to use the bathroom. Start it without me." I try not to let my eyes meet her skeptical gaze as I slip away from the picnic table and walk towards the house.

Aunt Rivka and Uncle Herb live in what my mother used to refer to as a modern house. All one story, clean, flat lines, big windows. I walk through the sliding glass door, through the den, past all the bowling trophies and photos of flushed faces at boozy parties. Aunt Rivka's hair is always perfect in these pictures as if she's managed to add a few spritzes of Aqua Net before each shot was taken. I see a picture of our whole family: my parents, my brothers and me, taken about five years ago. It's shoved way in the back of the shelf, covered with dust.

Ever since my parents divorced, no one mentions my father very often. Now, when we all get together as a family, it feels unbalanced, like a car traveling on three wheels.

Instead of going to the bathroom, I pick up the photo, go into their kitchen, open the refrigerator and take out a can of beer. Pabst Blue Ribbon. Christ, what a class act these two are. Not that I have much room to complain. I'd just spent my freshman year at college drinking the cheapest crap I could get my hands on. I open the can, take a long swallow and lean back against the counter. Why in hell did I come home for the summer? I could have stayed at school, worked part-time and come home when I felt like it. I could have taken a couple of classes. I could have spared myself this dose of reality.

I think about all my friends who are staying at school for the summer. Right about now they'd be sitting in the tall, damp grass by the reservoir, smoking a joint and eating Hostess cupcakes.

"Ruth! Ruthie!" My mother's shrill voice brings me out of the tall grass and back to the kitchen.

"I'm in here, Mom." I shove the photo behind my back so she won't catch me looking at it. Mom's not one for reminiscing. My mother walks into the kitchen wearing Espadrilles, a peasant blouse and a pair of floral print bellbottoms that are way too short.

"Why are you in here all by yourself, sweetie?" Her look is more accusatory than sympathetic, like I may have stolen the coffee maker and stuffed it into my shorts.

"I just needed to get out of the heat for a minute."

"Well, we miss you outside. Rivka's telling that silly story about when she and Herb ran into Marilyn Monroe in Niagara Falls on their honeymoon."

I roll my eyes. "I've heard it only about a million times."

She glares at me. "We've all heard it a million and *one* times. It gives Rivka pleasure to tell this story. You know how she loves an audience. Don't ruin this day for me, OK?"

Here it comes, I think. Here comes the reason I should have taken summer school classes. "I'll be right out, Mom. I just need to pee, OK?" I start to walk towards the bathroom.

"And don't use language like that, either. Nice girls say 'tinkle' instead."

I wait for my mother to close the screen to the sliding glass door before I return the photo to the den and go into the bathroom. Aunt Rivka's powder room, as she likes to call it, looks like something out of a New Orleans brothel. The wallpaper is green and gold with sketches of men and women dressed in some sort of peasant clothing. In some scenes, the men are chasing the women, and in others, the couples are engaged in what appears to be foreplay. In all the sketches, the women are very busty and are bursting out of their clothing. As I sit on the toilet I contemplate the various couples and try to make the correlation between foreplay and using the bathroom. I wonder if the wallpaper in Aunt Rivka's bedroom has drawings of people sitting on toilets or brushing their teeth.

The toilet has a fuzzy rug on top of the tank with a matching rug on the floor around the base. Both rugs are harvest gold and match the hand towels and the shell-shaped soaps arranged like a still-life in a shell-shaped dish on the sink. There is an overwhelming scent of air freshener coming from a dispenser, disguised as a vase of flowers, sitting on the top of the toilet tank. The smell makes me sneeze a few times as I flush the toilet and quickly wash my hands.

I open the bathroom door and hear Aunt Rivka through the screen telling the Niagara Falls story. I walk up to the screen door and peek out at everyone sitting around her at the picnic table. As she opens her mouth to speak, I close my eyes, remembering another time she told this story. I was about twelve-years-old and my father was cooking the steaks with Uncle Herb. They were making fun of Aunt Rivka and her obsession with telling this story. My father was laughing. We were all having a good time. We were balanced. Aunt Rivka's voice brings me back to the present.

"So, I walk up to Marilyn and ask her for her autograph but it's clear she's had a couple, you know what I mean, and she can hardly even hold a pen for God's sake. Herb told me to forget it but you know me, I couldn't just let an opportunity like that pass me by. So, I say to her 'Miss Monroe, I know you've had a busy day but would you mind terribly if I asked you to sign this napkin?' I had a cocktail napkin from this little joint on the Canadian side that served the best Manhattans. Remember that bar? What the heck was it called?"

Not waiting for Uncle Herb's answer, Aunt Rivka holds up a photo album to show a scrap of yellowed paper with some kind of scrawl on it, sticking out of the plastic sleeve. Next to it is a faded black and white photo of Aunt Rivka with her arm around a squinting and grinning Marilyn Monroe. Aunt Rivka's hair is perfect in the photo, despite the mist coming off the falls.

I walk back into the kitchen and prop myself up on the counter to savor my beer and my solitude. I could lip-synch the story from start to finish while Aunt Rivka tells it. In fact, I could lip-synch almost any story that any one of my family members tell. We seem to pride ourselves on repeat performances, as if we all have some sort of memory disorder where we forget a story as soon as it's told. I finish my beer, take a deep breath and head out to the backyard.

My three younger brothers have set up a croquet court and are slamming the balls into the redwood fence that runs along the perimeter of the yard, paying no attention to the location of the wickets. My mother and Aunt Rivka are on the side of the house, drinking scotch from plastic cups and sharing a cigarette like a couple of sneaky high school girls. Uncle Herb is cooking several large slabs of meat on a charcoal grill. He's wearing one of those aprons that says 'Kiss the Cook' and has a very satisfied grin on his face.

"How do you like your steak done, honey?" Uncle Herbs asks me.

"I've stopped eating meat." I practically whisper my reply, as if this is the first time I've said it out loud. It occurs to me that I hadn't bothered to tell anyone.

"What do you mean you've stopped eating meat? Since when?" My mother's ears have picked up my signal like a short-wave radio on a clear night. She marches over to where Uncle Herb and I are standing.

"I just don't like the taste of it anymore. It's no big deal. I can eat all the other stuff here." I point at the picnic table laden with potato salad, ambrosia salad, Velveeta slices and Ritz Crackers. I know my mother considers this latest dietary change a personal affront, like it's all about her. I think quickly how to build up my arsenal of answers for the upcoming interrogation.

"Are you hanging out with weirdoes at school? Are you spending time with musicians and Women's Libbers? Are you becoming one of those health nuts?"

My mother has a strange way of lumping groups of people together.

"Mom, it's not like that. I told you I just don't like the taste of it anymore." I can see that she's not buying my simple explanation.

"This is about your father, isn't it? You're still blaming me because of the divorce, aren't you? If he were here tonight...."

If he were here tonight I'd be eating the steak just like I always have. Dad was the one who made the steaks, Uncle Herb made the drinks and my mother and Aunt Rivka would sit on lawn chairs in the corner of the yard and gossip. That's what I remember. That's how I want it to be.

Uncle Herb tries to soothe my mother. "Betty, don't get all worked up about this. It's probably just a phase she's going through. You know how kids like to try new things in college."

My mother looks at me suspiciously. "Sometimes I just don't understand you, Ruth. Your uncle is making us a perfectly nice dinner and you are acting so disrespectful."

Uncle Herb tries to ease the tension by changing the subject. My mother stomps off to discuss my rebellious behavior with Aunt

Rivka, giving me a disgusted look as she turns around. Uncle Herb calls me over to him.

"C'mere, Ruthie honey, and tell your old Uncle Herb about your first year at school." Uncle Herb and I have never been close. He and Aunt Rivka didn't have any kids and he's always treated my brothers and me like he's trying to sell us something.

"It was OK. Exams were hard." I hear the words coming out of my mouth but I feel like I'm not really there.

"So how are your grades?" I can see he's trying to make casual conversation. He flips one of the steaks and I listen to the sizzle of the meat as it hits the grill.

I look up at him and instead of answering his question, I ask him this:

"Do you miss my father?"

Uncle Herb seems startled by the question.

"Of course, I miss him, honey, but you know the situation."

The smell of the seared meat makes me dizzy. Uncle Herb puts the spatula on top of each steak and presses down on them one at a time. The meat sizzles angrily. Wiping the sweat from his upper lip with the back of his hand, he checks the steaks as the silence hangs over us like smoke over the grill.

"Sometimes I don't feel like I belong here anymore."

Uncle Herb takes a long drink from his highball glass and looks at me like he's going to tell me about human reproduction. He sighs deeply.

"I know how you feel, honey. Sometimes I feel the same way."

We watch the steaks cooking for a few minutes, deep in our own thoughts.

"I'm feeling kind of dizzy. I'm going inside to wash my face." I walk away from Uncle Herb and go back into the house.

This whole evening feels wrong without my father. I find the family picture I saw earlier and take it back into the kitchen. The photo looks like it hasn't been dusted in years. I take a paper towel and clean the dust from the glass, my heart pounding as if I'm about to uncover a secret. My father looks happy in the picture, we all look happy. I study the photo trying to find some sort of clue in my parents' eyes but I only see blank, smiling faces. I return the photo to the shelf, walk out to the backyard and sit down at the picnic table.

My mother, my brothers, and Aunt Rivka are crowded around Uncle Herb waiting for him to cut the steak. I pick up a paper plate and walk towards the grill.

About the author:

Liz Morrison is a freelance writer living in San Diego. Her work has been published in *Sinister Wisdom, From These Walls* and on GenerationJ.com. Liz also writes feature stories and a monthly opinion column for San Diego's *Update* newspaper.

THE MESSAGE
©2001 by Gail Cauble Gurley

What we love is always near. It rests in our hearts, our minds,
our memories. —G. Gurley

JODIE RAN ACROSS the end of the expansive front porch,
easing by the large porch swing suspended from the ceiling where
she spent many happy hours on her visits, crossed the remaining
space and burst through the front door. She skipped over the wool
living room rug, worn thin from the front door to the door on the
opposite wall by countless feet and numerous decades.

As she entered the door, which was never locked, she shouted
eagerly, "Grandmother!"

"Yo," came her grandmother's reply from the kitchen.

Jodie rushed down the hall of what was once the dining room
to reach her grandmother in the kitchen. When Amanda Poole's
sons had returned from World War II they had closed up a large
portion of the existing dining room and installed a bathroom so as
to update the large home. Jodie didn't remember when it was a
dining room, but she did remember going outside to the
bathroom. This new room had been a welcomed addition.

She finally reached the warm embrace of her grandmother and
snuggled comfortably against the familiar texture of her worn,
cotton apron. Her aprons had bibs, which slipped over her head,
and sashes were tied sassily at the waist. They were created by
Amanda and included pockets trimmed with bright rick-rack.
Jodie always encountered the familiar apron when she entered the

house. Even on Sunday mornings before church, the apron would be tied securely over special dresses or suits until time to depart. It would be removed and hooked over a nail by the door as Amanda left the house, to be retrieved as soon as she returned from church several hours later.

Jodie's mother and younger sister made a more dignified entry behind her and arrived to an equally warm welcome. Jodie treasured her time with her grandmother and would always strive to arrive first so as to get the first generous hug.

Margaret and six-year-old Lynn left Jodie there while they went to the doctor for Lynn's pre-school physical examination and vaccinations before Lynn entered first grade. School began in four weeks so Jodie's visits were particularly precious now.

Jodie slipped quietly into the hallowed pantry, which was connected to the back of the kitchen. She felt that she was entering a special, almost holy, place when she descended the five wooden steps into the small, dark room. One tiny window at the west end of the room allowed the sun to cut through the dusty interior in long, smoky ropes. Jodie loved to brush her hand through the sun and watch the dust specks scamper and flutter about. These sun ropes would travel across the room throughout the afternoon, illuminating the treasures stored on the groaning shelves of bounty. Amanda tended a large vegetable garden and various fruit trees each year, and worked tirelessly to preserve these crops for the winter. Her philosophy was "Waste not, want not."

The sun was slicing across the delicious sweetness of preserves and jellies which were Jodie's favorites among the plenty. The plums sparkled like royal amethysts under the golden beam while the apple jelly was a bright, warm crimson, promising a sweet, delectable future treat. The strawberry was clouded by seeds but these tiny spots twinkled like stars under the sun's intrusion. Her favorite among the bounty, however, was the thick, ebony, sinfully rich blackberry jelly. When the rays reached these special treasures, the darkness in the jars looked like luxurious, opulent black velvet and Jodie's heart would soar and her mouth water at the memory of the decadent richness inside.

Just beyond the jars of delectable fruits sat the practical, sturdy offerings of canned vegetables. Corn, tomatoes, green beans, pickles and okra stood proudly, packed with vitamins and minerals and good health. Jodie scrunched up her nose slightly as the sun slipped across these essentials. The yellows, versatile greens and even rich reds were no match for the jewel tones of the fruited elixir of the jellies and preserves. She knew vegetables were good for her and were necessary to consume in order to reach the ecstasy of the sweet jars, but they were merely an unpleasantness she had to endure. The rule was no dessert until all her vegetables had been eaten.

She loved to follow Grandmother around the large kitchen as fruits and vegetables, which the two of them had gathered from the yard and garden, were washed and prepared for immediate consumption or future enjoyment. Amanda would sit on a stool by the kitchen window and snap, shell or peel while Jodie stood against her elbow, watching every move and helping when she could.

Amanda was a petite woman in her mid-60s with gray hair tied up in a neat bun resting on her neck. When she let it down to brush, it fell below her waist. She wore no makeup and never had. She had beautiful blue eyes that glittered with mirth and intelligence. Her hands and feet were twisted by arthritis but no one had ever heard her complain. It slowed her down a bit but certainly did not stop her. She wore long, practical dresses of faded cotton, dimmed by numerous washings as well as the hot North Carolina sun as they hung on the backyard clothesline to dry.

Her shoes were sensible, black leather, low topped so as not to cause discomfort to her twisted ankles, and were tied with a simple black shoestring. She wore hose rolled down below her knees in order not to hinder her bending and stooping as she worked but they were never visible as her dress reached below her shins. Jodie was enthralled by the shoes. When Amanda removed them, they retained the form of her misshapen feet, and Jodie would run her fingers over the lumps, bumps and occasional cut put there with a razor blade to allow swollen tissue to stretch.

Jodie was petite like her grandmother with the same large blue eyes. In addition to the intelligence emanating, there was a maturity and wisdom present that went well beyond Jodie's eight years. She soaked up everything her grandmother said, and like her grandmother, loved to read. She had a voracious appetite for books and frequently had her nose in one, as Grandmother would remark. Amanda had instilled a love of knowledge in all seven of her children as well as her twenty-one grandchildren.

Amanda and her late husband Tom had both gone to college. This was a very rare occurrence in 1906 America, especially for a woman. Amanda wanted to be a teacher and Tom dreamed of being an architect.

Two years into her education, Amanda's father died and she was forced to leave college. A year later, Tom's father died and he too left behind his dreams of being an architect. He became a carpenter, building strong, sturdy homes and built a small one to share with Amanda after their marriage. Shortly afterwards, the babies started coming, and Amanda stayed at home to care for them. She never regretted her fate, however, and thrived in the role of wife, homemaker, and mother as well as sometime music teacher on the pump organ in the front room. These lessons brought in much needed nickels and dimes through the years. She was equally successful as a grandmother and was deeply revered by her grandchildren.

The tiny house was expanded through the years as the family grew. Jodie had always known that rooms were added to the house and would frequently lie on the floor studying the ceilings and floors, trying to determine how the additions were joined. Tom was such an expert craftsman that it was extremely difficult to determine exactly where these add-ons occurred. He had died in 1937, so Jodie had never known him but studying the workmanship on the walls helped her feel close to his memory. He seemed to be alive in those very walls he had so lovingly crafted.

Jodie left the deliciousness of the pantry. "Grandmother!" she called out.

"I'm in the yard, Jodie," Amanda called back.

Jodie shoved the back screen door open, slamming it against the wall, bounded down the twelve wooden steps off the back porch, and rushed to her grandmother's side. She was on her knees at the flowerbed, digging into the rich earth and retrieving tiny flower bulbs.

Jodie was enchanted by her grandmother's flowerbed. There were numerous species and colors and aromas present throughout the year. Where Amanda was digging was the jonquil bed.

"What are you doing to the jonquils?" Jodie inquired.

"Thinning them out and moving some of the bulbs to another area."

"Why?"

"Because they're too thick and unless I thin them out, they won't bloom as well next spring." Amanda was amused by Jodie's curiosity. She sounded almost defensive of the bulbs. She was glad that Jodie loved her home so much. It validated Amanda's and Tom's presence and purpose on earth.

Jodie moved away from the jonquil bed to explore other areas of the yard. It was not a large yard but was well planned and well planted. In addition to the large umbrella shade trees that was the focal point, there was a large apple tree, a mature lilac bush, and a huge fig bush that grew up the side of the house and nestled under the kitchen window. The apples and lilacs were long gone but the figs were hard, green obelisks, waiting to ripen and release their sweet brown goodness.

Jodie's eyes rested on the mass of burgundy daisy mums just beginning to burst open among the iris leaves which stood guard at the property line beside the house next door. She loved to kneel among these rich jewels and rub her hands, arms, and face over their thickness. The pungent odor was not as pleasant as the butter yellow jonquils but was hardy, substantial, and earthy. She enjoyed weaving them together to make a regal crown for her head, and she knew that Grandmother would never scold her for breaking them off. She was careful not to pull the plants up by the root and only picked what she needed to make her crown or fill a vase.

"Why aren't any of these yellow, Grandmother?"

Amanda was caught off guard by the question but wasn't surprised. Yellow was Jodie's favorite color, and she would frequently bring into the house collections of various yellow flowers including wild buttercups, the happy jonquils when in bloom, and even dandelions peeking up through the grass.

"Well, they aren't yellow because they're red, Jodie," Amanda struggled to explain. "They've always been that color."

"Will they ever be yellow?"

"I don't think so, honey. The message to be red is in their roots and genes, and they'll always be that way." Jodie was disappointed but accepted the explanation and made no further mention of it.

Sundays were particularly pleasant for Jodie. After attending the Lutheran church in their small village of Charity, the whole family would meet at Amanda's house for lunch. Everyone would bring food and the long kitchen table would bow under the load of deliciousness set before the noisy, laughing crowd. Jodie would eat until she was near bursting.

The women would clean up while the men retreated to the comfortable, worn living room. The young would escape outside during the summer and into the front bedroom in cold weather. There were huge chests and an armoire in Amanda's room to hide in and tall beds and thick legged tables to hide under. Frequently, there would be a quilt frame set up with a quilt in progress, and it encompassed most of the room so they would play endless games of cowboys and Indians in teepees, or become kings and queens living a castle, or cavemen living in caves.

The years sped by and Jodie grew up as Amanda grew older. Jodie's love for her grandmother and all the treasured memories and activities at her home did not diminish, however. She felt no embarrassment because of her love for her grandmother nor did she consider that love unsophisticated, as did many of her more worldly peers.

As Amanda advanced in years, she remained busy and active, continuing to raise her garden, can her vegetables and make the delightful fruit preserves and jellies. She thrived on the continued love and devotion from her family, especially her grandchildren.

Jodie graduated high school and college, married, and moved an hour away from her beloved grandmother. However, she managed to visit her each weekend. She never left Amanda's house without a gift, and after they moved into their new home, Amanda would present various bulbs and plants she had dug out of the yard. Jodie would rush home with them and place them in a carefully selected spot of honor in the yard. Soon the small yard was filled with botanical offerings and became a miniature replica of Amanda's yard.

Each spring, Jodie would watch with eager anticipation until the first jonquils burst forth in their yellow beauty. Sometimes they bloomed in a late winter snow, and were always the first on the block to appear. The vintage flowers were more fragrant than the scientifically engineered ones from new bulbs at other homes on the block. Jodie's blossoms were smaller but would light up a room with their glory and fragrance.

In the fall, the long-awaited burgundy daisy mums would bloom, and each year they became thicker as the roots spread with proliferation. They were set in the upper corner of the back yard and cascaded regally down the hill. Jodie would sit below them in the warmth of the early fall sunshine, basking in their beauty and running her fingers through the buds. She enjoyed picking and weaving crowns for herself and for her daughter Mandy, Amanda's namesake. Like Jodie, Mandy spent many happy hours at the home of her great-grandmother, learning and laughing and loving.

In the year of her ninetieth birthday, Amanda began to fade. Jodie and Mandy made an extra effort to visit with her each weekend. The vegetable garden had long ago been abandoned and the beloved flowerbeds were matted with weeds and overgrowth. The succulent sweetness of the jellies and preserves was no more than a pleasant memory. Jodie and Mandy would dig in the dirt to remove weeds and thin out flowers choked by their own propagation.

Amanda watched sadly as she sat in a chair by the flowerbed. She longed to sink her fingers into the warm, moist earth and smell the rich, dark fertility she had worked in for so many years. She could see the tangles of roots and the occasional earthworm wriggling about, keeping the earth from becoming packed and adding food to the plants.

Jodie and Mandy were aware of her painful silence, and maintained a light and cheerful bantering as they worked. Jodie scooped up a double handful of the dirt and placed it gently in the lap of Amanda's apron. Her blue eyes, clouded by cataracts and age, sparkled with tears, love, and gratitude as she smiled warmly at Jodie. She pressed her hands into the soil and lifted it to her nose. She could not only smell the musty darkness but she could taste the richness. It was more delicious than any meal she had ever consumed.

In the late summer, Amanda suffered a massive cerebral hemorrhage. She managed to reach Margaret by telephone and ask for help. Margaret rushed to her after calling an ambulance, and accompanied her mother to the hospital. Later that evening after Amanda had stabilized, she called Jodie.

Jodie's heart lurched when she received the news from her mother, and she felt panicky, even after being assured that Amanda was resting comfortably. She knew without being told that this was the beginning of the end for her beloved grandmother.

Several weeks later, Amanda was moved into a nursing home. Jodie and Mandy continued their weekly visits, and Jodie would sit by Amanda's bed, reading the church bulletin to her, showing her family photographs and just holding her hand. Each time they left, Amanda would plead with them to take her home. Jodie felt helpless, standing on the edge of effectiveness, viewing the situation without hope.

The treasured burgundy daisy mums bloomed right on schedule that late September, and she gathered huge masses of them to place in Amanda's room. Amanda was getting weaker but she always recognized them and managed a smile when Jodie or Mandy entered. She eventually became too weak to speak but managed to raise her hand to touch them in a greeting of welcome.

In early November, with the season's final bouquet of Jodie's mums by her bedside, Amanda Poole quietly slipped away.

Jodie was in deep despair, moving numbly through the funeral and the days and weeks following. She knew that her life would never again be the same. She had not only lost her beloved grandmother, her friend and mentor, but she had lost her childlike innocence regarding life. She had never before lost a loved one and even though she certainly knew what death was, it had never struck so close to her heart before.

Winter passed and spring arrived. The jonquils exploded, their yellow crowns bobbing happily in the not yet warm sun of the North Carolina March. Jodie placed them on Amanda's grave, weeping quietly and sadly. She was unable to shake this emptiness reaching into the very cellars of her heart and soul.

The summer sweltered that year and Jodie couldn't bring herself to work in the mums. She knew they needed to have weeds pulled out, but the grief, not the heat, kept her away from that corner of the yard.

Summer waned and early fall arrived. The leaves were particularly beautiful that year. The trees were adorned with vibrant yellows, reds, purples and oranges in hues that Jodie never remembered seeing before. Autumn had always been Jodie's favorite season, and frequently as she was driving home from work that year, she would be so overcome with the breathtaking glory of the colors that she would pull off the street, step outside the car, and just soak in the majesty of it all. More than once she thought, "I wish Grandmother could see this."

October was speeding by and still Jodie procrastinated against approaching the mums. One bright, unusually warm Saturday afternoon common to fall in the South, she moved slowly up the concrete driveway beside her home, passed the clothesline, and found herself being pulled across the backyard toward the daisy mum garden.

As she neared the site she stopped, frozen in place. She gasped in disbelief as she viewed the profusion of blooms. Never had she seen them so thick and lush but that wasn't what took her breath away. The familiar dark burgundy flowed across the patch, but about three quarters of the way through, the burgundy began to fade and lighten to paler amber, then beige and then another breathtakingly unexplainable color. As the garden ended, the blooms were no longer burgundy but had gradually become a beautiful, clear golden yellow which was pure in its clarity. There was no hint of burgundy, amber or beige contaminating these beautiful mums.

Jodie cried out in joy, disbelief, and sheer ecstasy as she felt the bonds of grief burst and fall away from her heart. Her grandmother had sent a loving message that she was fine and still loved Jodie. There was no need to worry or grieve anymore. The feeling of love and compassion in Grandmother's message nearly overwhelmed Jodie, and the tears splashing on these flowers were no longer tears of pain but tears of gratitude and love and relief.

She buried her face in the yellowness and wrapped her fingers around the petals and stems. She slipped a crown of yellow over her red hair and filled her lap with their purity. She filled every vase in her house and loaded masses of them into the car for the trip to the cemetery. They adorned Amanda's grave as Jodie thanked her for sending this special message.

The mums never again bloomed yellow but returned to their original burgundy the next year. That fact only reinforced Jodie's certainty that she had been comforted by this special gift from Grandmother. Jodie was at peace.

About the author:

Gail published a collection of inspirational short stories entitled *Tales From the Sunroom* in 2001. It has been well accepted and acclaimed. Her new novel entitled *The Bird House: A Gift of Hope* was released in December 2002. It is an inspirational story of a young family in New York during the Great Depression and their struggles to survive. Reviews on this latest work have been excellent. She resides in North Carolina with her husband of 32 years. They have a daughter and three grandchildren in Houston, TX. She earned a B. A. in psychology and an M. Ed in education from the University of North Carolina at Greensboro. Writing has been the realization of a lifelong dream, and she credits her success to the encouragement and support she has received from her family and many friends.

HITTING ON WOMEN
©1999 by Charles L. McDermott

A FEW MONTHS ago, my wife took me out for dining and dancing. The food was first-rate, and so was the live band playing popular and mostly slow dance songs. It was sponsored by Cindy's women's organization and the ladies were dressed-up. They were all checking each other out to see what design, style and color the other women wore. I think they were also checking to see if their friends got everything fitted into their dress. I see my 'Sweet and Sassy' wife looking over my left shoulder, and Cindy almost gasps. "Would you look at that?"

Since I obey my wife, I turned and was face to face with a very attractive woman, maybe a decade younger than Cynthia, but it wasn't her age or good looks that got my wife's attention. It was her very low-cut dress that barely contained her breasts. There was unbelievable cleavage from my position about three feet away, but I was drawn forward and downward to where I was no more than a foot from the feature attractions. 'Magnificent Seven,' I strongly exclaimed. My wife immediately pulled me away as the Bosom Beauty in Blue asked for an explanation.

"Madam, I couldn't tell if they were 36's or 38's, so I split the difference, they are magnificent," I added. She smiled, but Cindy gave me an elbow in the ribs that would have caused any NBA Basketball Player to be ejected.

Why is it when the occasion seems okay to hit on women, men are always getting into trouble? Let me give you an example. Not long ago my wife told me that I never say anything nice to her little sister. The wife says that Sissy (a.k.a. Amanda) will be over in a couple of hours with a new pair of 'huggies' (blue jeans), 'do' (haircut/hair set or do), and 'nails' (trim/clean/polish fingernails). "Charlie, please pick at least one item, and say something nice to Sissy. Make her feel good!" Cynthia spells it out.

When Amanda came over we had a polite conversation, but there was nothing I could say from my heart to compliment her on. Then she turned her back to me, walked a few feet to our coffee table, and bent over to browse through some magazines. At that moment, I felt my wife's request could be honored. "Mandy, those jeans...those jeans..." my words just stumbled out.

"Charlie, these are just my 'work down on Friday' jeans."

"Mandy, with your butt, you could stop traffic *any* day of the week, and work down both sides of the street." I meant to pay Amanda a compliment, but before her sister could respond, my spouse kicks me in the shin with the force of a NFL field goal kicker.

"That was only an attention-getter, Charlie; I will deal with you later."

A few months before the Amanda incident, my wife and I met at one of the nicer fast food establishments for lunch. My mate sees a friend of hers, and invites Terri to join us. Terri and my misses were Sorority Mates at the University, but I've only known her a couple of years. What I do know is that Terri is a fine-looking woman. She pulls out a chair and sits down; then Terri turns toward me. "Charlie, what do you think of my new sweater?" Terri asked a straightforward question, and this lady definitely points forward.

"Terri, I don't know much about sweaters, but you sure do have a fine set of knockers pushing up against that sweater."

Terri blushes, but not that much. I think she probably expected me to say something like that. "Charlie, shut your mouth! Terri has been married longer than we have, their two girls are both in middle school, and she was just recommended for full partnership in her law firm. We'll talk more about this tonight." Cindy lets me have both barrels. (How could I have forgotten about Terry's other qualifications?)

'Angel on my pillow, and frequent devil on my navel' was polite and restrained when we first revisited the Terri sweater comments after supper. Then the pace picked up. "Charlie, it's getting to where I'm scared to have you around any of my friends or relatives for fear you'll try to hit on them," my wife complained.

"Maker of our marvelous children, and you do make me wild on Saturday night, let me swear to you that I would never hit on your friends and kin. To be honest, there're very few that I would even throw a rock at."

"Sometimes you're a super spouse, but tonight we will be apart. Let me introduce you to our sofa. It's a pullout, with sheets, blankets and pillow at your fingertips."

Cindy knows I will begin to brood. I will remember, and start to meditate about my sin: 'Hitting on Terri.' I do remember that Terri is a fine-looking woman. I didn't make Terri fine looking, but since she is—why can't I tell her?

There's a limit to what should be said to any woman in public. A few months ago, Biff, a regular at the sports bar I frequent, was eyeing this blonde fox who was with two of her lady friends. Single women at a sports bar should expect more hitting than at a coat-and-tie cocktail bar. Biff went a bit past 'woman hitting'—a huge bit past! Biff looked up one side of the blonde and down the other side. He was leering and drooling the whole time. Every now and then he would add an easily understood: 'Yes!' Biff kept repeating this same routine. The Blonde waited until the waitress brought Biff a new beer, and then walked over to his table.

Ms 'Tender but Tough' went up to Biff, and put her hands on his fresh mug. "May I?" The Golden Blonde asked in a sweet voice. Biffs eyes opened wide as he nodded 'yes.' The lovely and not intimidated woman, picked up his mug, and poured the contents over Biff's head. "I guess you were just as thirsty as you were crude." Biff left, and the whole bar cheered.

"That's one small mug for womanhood, and a mug that good men don't need," yelled an attractive brunette sitting two tables away who jumped up to add her support. Biff got no sympathy at that sports bar that night. The message was very clear that men desiring female company best remember some basic manners.

A few days later, my mother called for me to take her to the nursing home to see her Aunt. Mom is sixty-three, and Aunt Sue must be in her mid-eighties. "Aunt Susan you look great and I love that color in your cheeks. Did you chase the gardener all week?" Mom started the compliments.

"Hush, Mabel. I haven't been chasing anybody, and if I caught somebody, what would I do with them?" Aunt Sue replied.

"If you've lived over eighty years, and don't know what to do with a man, you'll just have to stay around for another eighty. Now what have you been up to?"

Now comes Aunt Sue's ten-page computer printout list from memory of her tribulations including bad health, bad service and bad food. Mom listens, but every few minutes she interrupts to describe an attractive male resident on West ward or how nice Aunt Sue's hair is, and what lovely colors are in her blouse.

"Mom, you really laid it on thick with Aunt Sue today, didn't you?" I asked later.

"Son, women like to be told they are attractive to others, and especially to men. Many elder men and women remain very romantic, and they have quite satisfying sexual relationships. The important role for me, and for most of my friends, is to maintain an appearance and attitude to interest men, and maybe to attract one to stay a while."

"Mom, you're saying that it's very important for every woman to keep her honey pot attractive at all times for her public. In addition, part of a women's nature is to attract a male bee to the vicinity of her honey from time to time, whether she ever sees his stinger or not. Is that about it, Mom?"

"You win the 'crude award', son—but you're basically correct.

We need to know that we're seen and accepted as an attractive woman. This may not be a good example, but a queen bee goes through quite a ritual before mating, and when it's over, it's really over for her lover. There is similarity among animals and humans, but as humans we have a brain and a soul. Son, men have the chance to make women feel good about themselves. Please take advantage of every opportunity to compliment women."

"Mom, thanks for explaining that women need compliments. I would appreciate if you would go over this with Cynthia sometime. My wife thinks my attempts to compliment her friends and kin are just opportunities to tease her or make her jealous."

"Son, that's a good idea. To be fair should I secretly videotape you making compliments to women? Then Cindy and I could watch, and discuss at the same time."

"Mom, don't rush into a conversation with Cindy; you're so busy and all. I'll find some additional time with the wife, and have a full and frank discussion."

Those at the lower rungs need many compliments, but I just cannot see me doing that. How could you tell a seventy-year-old woman that her butt has more moves than a Ping-Pong ball in a tight match? The way I see it, if a woman looks sharp or exciting, I will be more than glad to pass on the compliments.

Cindy is off the mark telling me not to compliment attractive women. They want to be complimented just like all the other women. Both my mother and wife have reinforced that women want compliments, but how can I do it? How can I do it safely? This is a question that married men have pondered throughout modern times.

Everybody in the company has a computer. Some of the folks in Design have two or three. To support our hundreds of computers, we have a computer support department that installs new computers, repairs old ones and modifies or adds new computer software as required.

The department is run by a woman in her thirties assisted by two women in their twenties. There's some help from college interns in the summer, and during Christmas and Spring breaks, but the department is pretty much on their own most of the year. They're next to Shipping, and that's where I was heading. I try to look in the computer room when I pass by, since I have an interest in computers.

When I get to Computer Support, their doors are closed. I can never remember the doors being closed in the past. I hear noises. When I get closer, the noise level increases; it sounds like several women panting. That is exactly what it is!

There're two or more women panting and groaning. If there is one thing that drives me crazy, it's to hear a woman panting, and for me to be on the other side of the door. These women might be in serious difficulty and it's my duty to help. "This is Charlie and I'm coming in."

Once inside, I see the boss lady in the back working on her computer. Karen and Angela, the young and well constructed assistants, are standing by the door looking calm and cool. "What's the problem? I heard noises. Is something wrong? Can I help?"

"Charlie, we really could use some help. Women can have babies but it's you men who have the big muscles. We received twelve oversized monitors in yesterday, and need to record the serial numbers, and get them issued. They're too big and awkward for us to handle. Could you give us a hand?" Angela explains in her sweetest voice.

These women probably set me up, since my reputation does proceed me, but even if it was a coincidence, I've been had. To rush in their computer room as a macho male to help the 'panting women,' and then leave as a wimp who can't do heavy lifting would be my 'hitting on women death sentence.' "Angela, where would you like me to start? By the way, when these monitors start getting heavy, and I start to pant, who is going to call my wife?"

"Charlie, I will do it myself, and I'll tell Cynthia just what a good 'panter and gasper' you really are!" Karen responded.

"Why don't we forget my wife? You can just call 911 for my

emergency rescue." When I finished, I was almost ready for an Emergency Rescue, but I just turned and headed toward the door. "Would you mind telling me how you pulled this off?" I asked.

As I reached the door, I stopped to look at Karen and Angela. Neither spoke, and their jaws were locked tight, with each wearing a grin. Had their mouths opened, a huge laugh would've erupted. Angela and Karen just shook their heads, while I quietly left.

"Why am I the one to run around, and hit on women? Why can't women hit on me occasionally?" I asked myself an important question.

"Charlie, could it possibly be that you don't have, or you don't display, what women would like to hit on?"

"Kim, I didn't realize I was talking out loud. Those gals in Computer Support just worked me over."

"Charlie, come over to the break area, and tell me all about it. Sit down, and give me the skinny. I want to know everything about how these twenty-five-year-old built like 'twin brick out-houses' just sexually assaulted you."

"Kim, you are really hitting below the belt now."

"Horny silver hair, since you are one of my nine bosses, I will make this as gentle as possible. 'Hitting below the belt,' you say? Charlie, below your belt is the one area that you need not worry about any woman in this company ever visiting."

"Kim, your cutting me is not unusual. Hitting me with a shovel is. Are you having problems with your main steady?"

"Yes, I am and I don't want to talk about it. I am sorry, but it was pretty ugly".

"Understood. When you are in more of a talking mode, give me a read on women attacking Charlie."

"We can talk now, I just didn't want to talk about my situation. In a word, Charlie, you come on too strong; you need to slow down, and low down. Don't walk right up and say anything good or bad. Before you slam, back off. Even when you say something nice, don't stand nose to nose or navel to navel. Try to find other things about a woman to compliment her on, besides her B and B. If you want to put a smile on a woman's face, and a twinkle in her eyes, just tell her she's doing a damn fine job."

"Thank you, I appreciate the advice, especially when you had big problems." I watch Kim as she gets up from the table, turns and heads for her office. "Kim, you know you have a real fine...personality." I felt the need to make an appropriate compliment.

"Charlie, that is better. That's much better!"

I think I'm making progress. I got some good advice from my Mom, my wife and from Kim. 'Safe hitting' seems to be as much form as substance. All women wish to be complimented, and Charlie sure wants to compliment good looking women. Maybe Kim is correct. Sometimes, I may come on a bit too strong.

I am experienced with language to describe a woman's body, but I don't know enough about a woman's hair, fragrance, dress, jewelry or anything else to determine whether this should be complimented or not. When my wife asks an opinion on how something looks or smells on her, I always say, "Great!" How would I know? Do I need to go to fashion and charm school?

'Hitting in slow motion,' with little or no suggestive side, could be acceptable to women, from college coeds to Aunt Sue's friends. It's likely that neither a coed at half my age nor seniors, at double my years, would sense any sexual come-on. Unfortunately, this town has only one small college, and many retirement and nursing homes.

I knew it would happen; it had to. Charlie was asked to hit on a nice-looking woman, his own age. Talent is recognized. We have a joint marketing agreement with a small company to distribute and market some of our products that only have small market shares. They're located across town, and I visit their offices once a month. It's usually after one o'clock when I head back, and I stop along the way for a late lunch.

For the last three months, I've eaten at a family restaurant with great food and a cashier who is funny and sharp-looking. To pay my bill last time, I pulled out all of the bills and coins I had, and dropped them on the counter. The cute cashier counted them, and when it was correct to the penny, she remarked: *"Sir, you are good!"*

"Pretty Lady, it has been far too long since an attractive young woman told me that."

"Sir, you have been hitting on me for months, and you do it with class. We both enjoy it, and both know nothing will ever happen."

"Hold on, Sweet Young Thing. I may be old and haven't won you yet, but I ain't dead either."

"Just park it a minute; it's Charlie? Please listen to me for just a second. I want you to hit on my Mom. Charlie, it could mean a whole lot to her."

"Hard to tell what it'd mean to your Mom, but I know what it would mean to me. Serious injury, and maybe dismemberment! My best hope would be sleeping in the back yard for months. Didn't you see my wedding ring that I always wave around?"

"Charlie, shut up! This restaurant was built and run by father and his brother. Mom is the chef and a partner since Dad died a year and half ago. If you find me attractive, you should've seen Mom before Dad got sick. She's a good mother and a great chef, but the restaurant has become her life. She doesn't want to feel and look like the woman she had been. I just want you to throw some serious trash at her when you come by." Maggie was making a serious request.

"Charlie, I promise there's something in it for you. I won't report you to the pervert police. By your smile, I see it's time to meet my Mom, and here she comes now."

As her mother walked toward us, the resemblance between the two was striking. Her Mom had finished three hours of cooking, and supervising meal preparations in a hot kitchen; plus her cooking whites didn't showcase her figure, but Maggie's Mom was an attractive woman.

"I am so glad to meet your sister, Maggie. It is your older sister? You can't be Maggie's mother. I will have to shake my head, because the laws of this state clearly prohibit girls marrying under the age of fourteen and having babies." I greeted her Mom.

"Get out of here. Maggie, has this character paid for his meal or do I take him in the back, and get Silver Hair to wash the lunch dishes?" The Mom, and chef, responds.

"Mom, he paid in full, including a tip."

"I bet he paid by check. Let me see it."

"I think Mom wants your telephone number."

"Maggie, of course I do. I want his wife to pick him up before you and I take him out for the wildest time of his life. Charlie, I am glad to meet you. This is the third time I've seen you visiting with my little girl. You almost seem harmless."

"Anne, with an 'e'? Can I ask a favor? If I know my schedule a couple of days in advance, can I get that meatloaf? I have never had anything that good in my life."

"Charlie, if you call Maggie twenty-four hours in advance, you can not only order meatloaf when you get here, but I will be the one to personally bring the meal out to your table," Anne promised.

I had to go back to work, but without saying a word, Maggie grabbed my hand for a warm squeeze as I headed for the door. For a brief moment I had visions of checking all the restaurants, to see if there were other cashiers and cooks like Maggie and Anne.

What should I do, now that I am getting a lot better at hitting on women, and even becoming somewhat kinder and gentler? What I should do, is work to improve my hitting on Cindy and her friends and relatives. My Mom, Maggie and her Mom, and even Kim have tried to tell me that complimenting women is important. It's not just the compliment, but *how* the compliment is made that means so much to women.

I could pay attention to the compliments or remarks that women make about men and other women before deciding something to say. Simple compliments about her hair, fragrance, and outfit wouldn't be difficult when the compliment seems real to me.

Remarks about 'B and B,' other body parts, or a female's locomotion must take a nose-dive, except for my beautiful wife; those compliments should increase.

Mom called me to take her on another visit to see Aunt Susan. My mother is the woman who knows me better than anyone, including Cindy. As I got older, it was even more apparent my Mom was always in closer touch with people, and their feelings than I was. Maybe this explains why she would be my best friend— even if we weren't related.

As we headed to the nursing home, Mom repeated her warning, and gave a general pep talk on being nice to women. I tried several times to tell her my ways were already changing. "Mom, you have already made your point."

"Son, every week we visit Aunt Sue and her friends, is a week off her time on this planet. Please try to think first, and then say something to make all these ladies feel good." The only thing I could do was turn to Mom, nod my head, and smile. After we settled in Aunt Sue's room, I took the lead in making Aunt Sue and others in the nursing home feel good as women.

"Aunt Sue, where did you get that fire bright, red blouse? Isn't that a new hair set? You look mighty nice, but when we leave, I am going to lock you in, to keep those wild men from West Ward from having their way."

"Charlie, this is my aunt you are talking about, I can still wash your mouth out with soap. Now you go ahead and apologize," Mom said.

"I apologize, Aunt Sue. I won't lock the door. You can fend for yourself. Just don't call for help if you take on more than one at a time!" Mom was doing her best to hold back a smile, but Aunt Sue didn't even try to hold back a grin, and then a good laugh.

"Charlie, I know you are more full of it than a dozen Christmas turkeys, but if you only meant just a tiny part, that still sounded mighty good!"

Mom and I spent an hour at the home, taking turns giving 'hitting compliments' to Aunt Sue and her friends. As we walked to the car, my mother asked me what I thought. "Mom, I feel good. I really do. I think we made a difference in these women's day, and we enjoyed doing it.

Mom, we deserve a nice reward. We should celebrate with a good meal. Where are my Social Security taxes going to take us for lunch? Italian? Chinese? Seafood? Hold on, Mother of Mine, this lunch is on me. I am treating. We're going to a fine family restaurant with a fine-looking cashier."

"Son, if you are going somewhere to look at another woman, much less hit on her, Cindy and I will take turns beating your brains in." My Mom made a promise.

"Just hold on, Mom, just wait! You will love this restaurant and the cashier, and you will also love her mother!"

Will Charlie completely quit hitting on good-looking women, other than his wife? Will he limit his compliments of female body parts to his wife only? Charlie seems to be making progress, but he never said he was losing his eyesight, and never promised to become a saint!

About the author:

Charles L. McDermott, born and raised in Mobile, Alabama, began verbally composing stories even before starting school, where disrupting classes became a vocation for him. His elementary years required six different schools: three due to family relocations, the other three because he was "asked" to relocate. Things improved in high school, however, and Charles received honors and a Chemistry Degree in college. He went to Vietnam and was shot at. Fortunately, the bullets missed. It was then back to college for an MBA, and for the last eighteen years he was employed as a civilian at an army base near his hometown of Aberdeen, MD. His wife, tiring of his talking about story ideas and claims that he could write, bought him a computer and unloaded a shoebox of story ideas. To date, Charles has written thirty-two short stories, five novellas and final drafts of two novels. Women play a prominent role in his writings, displaying sweetness and sadness, while wrapped with tons of spice. His short story "Why I Want to be a Woman" was published by Writer Works in the spring as part of a short story collection.

CLOSE TO HOME
©2000 by Paul Perry

LEENA MAE CUMMINGS, guard on Cell Block F for fourteen years, was standing by Evelyn Smith's cell when the warden came walking down the long corridor that led to Evelyn's cell, her shoes echoing on the metal floor. She stopped in front of Evelyn's cell, leaned against the bars, looked in at the small gray-haired woman sitting on her bunk, head bent over a cigar box. "Is she about ready?" the warden asked Leena Mae.

Leena Mae shrugged heavy shoulders. "She's still sorting through stuff to keep and stuff to throw away. She's just got that Boston bag that she had when she came here and she's got more than will fit in it."

The warden frowned. "It's time to go Evelyn. You should have been out of here two days ago. You got to hurry it up."

Evelyn looked up at the big woman wearing the black pants suit, white blouse, horn-rimmed glasses almost concealing sharp blue eyes. "I'm just about ready, Warden. I just got to sort through this box here, mostly stuff some of the girls left me when they got out. This is all that's left. I gave my romance novel collection to Cookie and all of my movie star pictures to Sis." She looked around the tiny cell at the bare gray walls, sighed. "It sure looks sad in here without all my pictures."

The warden motioned for Leena Mae to unlock the cell door then she went inside, stopped in front of Evelyn and looked down at her. Her hair was a smooth iron gray, cut short, and the warden could see the pink of the scalp where the hair was a little too thin. "Well, Evelyn," she said, surprised to find herself reaching down to touch the woman's shoulder, "you got to be out of here by six p.m. and it's after five now. You can't stay here one more night. I already let you stay longer than I should have."

Evelyn looked up at the warden, her lips pressed together. Her eyes were red-rimmed but their color was a clear, pale gray. She looked to be in her mid- or late-fifties except when she closed her mouth, as she was doing now. Then she looked to be at least seventy. She sniffed, rubbed at her cheeks. "My stomach's still bothering me, Warden"

The warden sat down on the bunk near her, gave her a stern look. "The doctor said whatever it was that was hurting you, he couldn't find any cause of it." She stood up, walked to the cell door. "The last bus that'll take you to the halfway house leaves at six, Evelyn. I want you down to the discharge office in thirty minutes." She went out and closed the door behind her, pushed it until she heard the click of the lock. "When you're ready, Mrs. Cummings here will bring you down." She started away then stopped, looked back. "And wear your dentures, Evelyn. And put on that gray dress. Hurry up now." And she walked away, ignoring the mournful sigh coming from inside the cell.

Leena Mae leaned against the cell door, said to Evelyn, "You heard her. Let's get a move on now. If we don't show up in thirty minutes, she's going to be mad at both of us." Leena Mae was a big woman, looked fat with her stomach protruding over her navy-blue trousers, the short sleeves of her pale blue shirt fitting like sausage skins over her upper arms, but there was a lot of muscle under the fat.

When Leena Mae had first come to work as a guard at the women's prison in north Texas, the inmates had looked at her plump body and at the pleasant smile on her round brown face and they'd thought that they were going to have a pushover. But when a fight broke out in the mess hall about a month after Leena Mae's arrival, and Leena Mae had not only broken it up but had broken the arm of one of the fighters in the process, a one hundred and sixty pound member of the "Biker Chicks" motorcycle gang, the inmates had all decided to treat her with more respect, especially after they saw the ferocious look that had momentarily replaced the sweet smile, saw the sharp gleam in the dark brown eyes.

Leena Mae waited another ten minutes, watching Evelyn pull on a gray dress that hung loosely on her small, thin frame, then she opened the cell door with the key attached to her belt. "Time to go, hon," she said, standing aside, motioning for Evelyn to join her.

Evelyn nodded, picked up the battered Boston bag that contained all her worldly possessions. She looked up at Leena Mae. "I'm ready, I guess," she said. "I just dumped all that stuff in the waste basket there. No need to keep any of it, I guess."

As they walked through the dark corridor toward the front part of the prison, Leena Mae looked down at the little woman beside her, remembered again what another guard had told her when she first went to work on Block F. "She was some trouble when she came here, real standoffish, so some of the other women didn't like her, kind of gave her a hard time until word got around about what she had done to get forty-years-to-life."

Leena Mae and Carol, an older redheaded guard who dipped snuff, had been standing in the mess hall, watching the women eat, keeping an eye out for trouble. Leena Mae had noticed the little woman who always sat by herself, although once in a while one of the older inmates would stop by, say something to her, maybe pat her on the shoulder. She watched the woman take tiny bites of mashed potatoes and peas then turned and asked Carol, "What did she do?"

"Killed her husband with a crowbar. The way I heard it, she pounded him into a pulp." Carol carried a little Styrofoam cup and she spit into it. "She lived way out in the sticks in east Texas. Got forty-to-life back around nineteen-sixty."

Leena Mae's curiosity had been aroused. Her oldest son was

taking computer classes at City College in Houston and she asked him to see if he could find out anything about it. When he came to visit on the weekend, he said he found quite a bit from March and April of 1958. Evelyn Bains had taken a crowbar to her husband after he hit her. "It sounded like to me he did this a lot," Leena Mae's son, Gerard, told her. "I guess she finally got fed up and grabbed the crowbar. When they asked her in court why she hit him at least fifty times, she said, 'He just kept on moving.'"

The two of them had been sitting in Leena Mae's living room drinking orange Gatorade, watching the Cowboys get beat. "It don't seem like she should have got forty years for that," Leena Mae said.

Gerard shrugged. "Well, her husband was a county sheriff's deputy and she got tried by a bunch of people that lived out in that part of the country. And it sounded like she didn't do much to help herself when they tried her. She sat there with no expression on her face, according to the papers."

When Leena Mae and Evelyn arrived at the discharge office, they went in and sat down on plastic chairs just inside the door. "We got to wait here for the warden," Leena Mae told Evelyn. The old woman nodded, sat there looking uneasy. Sitting there beside the old woman, Leena Mae recalled the time, eight years ago, when Evelyn had come up for parole. Leena Mae had been one of the guards on duty in the room where the parole board met and she stood in the back of the room, watching Evelyn.

Evelyn had sat in front of the three members of the parole board, sitting stiffly in a wooden chair, and when the heavyset gray-haired woman who sat in the middle asked Evelyn if she had any kind of job she could go to on the outside, Evelyn had just shook her head. A thin black man sitting to the woman's left had leaned forward, asked Evelyn, "Could you ever kill again?" And she had said, without even thinking about it, "If I had to." That had been enough right there.

Two years ago, when she had come up for parole again, Leena

Mae hadn't been on duty, hadn't even had to be there that day, but she showed up to see if Evelyn would do better. But it went about the same way, Evelyn saying about the same things, with the same result.

But two months ago, when Evelyn's forty years were almost up, Leena Mae had volunteered to be on duty in the room where the parole board met. She knew the parole board could keep Evelyn in prison, even though she had almost served forty years, and she was concerned about what Evelyn was going to do. So, she couldn't hold back a smile when the warden showed up, spoke before Evelyn was asked any questions. "We've got a halfway house she can go to," the warden told the three board members, "and there's a nursing home not far from the halfway house where she can help out, make some money, eventually be able to support herself."

The warden had cleared her throat, looked uncomfortable. "Most people don't realize we've got our own nursing home right here in the prison. We've got three women with Alzheimer's, two others that are just senile. When they don't have any place to go, we just take care of them the best we can until they die." She sighed, looked down at Evelyn. "Evelyn here has been helping take care of them for the last three or four years. She's good at it."

Then the warden paused, a frown on her face, "I know she got forty-to-life but there's no need to keep her here any longer. Besides," she said, shrugging, "we're way overcrowded. We need her cell."

So, without Evelyn saying a word, even though she looked like she wanted to, the parole board decided that forty years was enough time for her.

When the warden came striding into the discharge office, she looked down at Evelyn and said, "You remember how to take the bus to get to the halfway house?"

Evelyn stood, along with Leena Mae. "Yes, ma'am. And I got my bus fare ready."

The warden nodded, held out her hand. "Well, good luck to you."

Evelyn stared at the warden's hand, a stunned look on her face. Finally, she reached out, took the hand gingerly, gave it a brief shake. She turned toward the door then hesitated, looked back at the warden. "I'm kind of worried about Louise and Marcie and the others."

The warden patted her on the shoulder. "They'll be all right, Evelyn. Now you get going." She looked at Leena Mae. "You can stay with her until she's on the bus."

"Yes, Warden," Leena Mae said, smiling. "I'll get her on her way."

They walked through the last guarded gate then out to the long walkway that led to the road that ran in front of the prison. There was a bus stop about two blocks down and Leena Mae walked Evelyn down to the bus stop, sat with her on the wooden bench there. She looked over at Evelyn, shook her head. "Don't you want to take that jacket off, Evelyn? It's August and I'm sweating up a storm in just my shirt and pants."

The jacket was a sky-blue Windbreaker, looked like it had been worn by more than one person over a number of years. Evelyn shook her head. "I've got them tattoos on my arms, from when I was bunking with Leeta." She stopped talking, looked down at her hands.

The bus pulled up half an hour or so later and Leena Mae stood there, watched Evelyn climb the stairs and hold out a bill to the driver. Evelyn went back and sat down by the window, waved at Leena Mae as the bus pulled away, then turned to look back at the prison as the bus rolled down the street and around a corner. Leena Mae stood there for a while, looking down the empty street, then she sighed and headed back to the prison.

Three days later, when Leena Mae was driving her '83 Monte Carlo to the prison for her day shift, she saw someone sitting on the bus stop bench. It was a little before six a.m. and still half-dark so Leena Mae was right in front of the bus stop before she saw that it was Evelyn. She was sitting stiffly, staring down the road toward the prison. She was wearing the same clothes she had been wearing three days earlier, including the blue Windbreaker.

Leena Mae parked, walked across the street and sat down beside her. "Okay, Evelyn," Leena Mae said, "just what are you doing sitting out here?"

Evelyn turned to look at her. She just stared at Leena Mae, shaking her head. Finally, she said, "They just roll them out on gurneys in the morning, out in this long dark hallway and they just leave them there all day. The doctor comes around about mid-morning, just walks from one gurney to another, checking their pulses to make sure they're alive, tells the nurses what medicine to give them to keep them doped up."

Leena Mae leaned her arm against the back of the bench, bent to look into Evelyn's eyes. "You all right, Evelyn? What in the world are you talking about anyway?"

"That nursing home where they sent me to help out. All they had me doing was emptying bedpans, changing diapers. Said I wasn't a nurse so that's all I could do." She looked up at Leena Mae. "One of them died out there one morning and they didn't even know it until they wheeled her back to her room that night." She paused, pressed her lips together. "I didn't go back there the next day," she said.

The sun was coming up now and already it was getting warm, humid. Leena Mae wiped her hand across her forehead, looked at Evelyn's lined face. "So, what are you doing here? There's no way the warden's going to let you back in the prison, Evelyn. You've got to know that."

Evelyn nodded. "I just thought . . .well, I thought if I talked to her, she might have some kind of job for me, maybe helping take care of the women in the infirmary."

Leena Mae stood. "Well, I'll get you in there to talk to her, but I don't think your chances are good."

The warden led them into her office. She had a big wooden desk, a gray metal file cabinet, two straight chairs with padded seats, and that was about it. There was a view of the prison yard from her window and Leena Mae could see only a couple of guards out there, walking together toward a door leading into the cellblocks. The warden told Leena Mae and Evelyn to sit down then she sat behind her desk, leaned forward to frown at Evelyn. "So, the job didn't work out?"

Evelyn shifted nervously in her chair. "No, ma'am. I . . .I just didn't like that place, the way they treated them old people."

The warden shook her head. "Well, I can't give you a job here, Evelyn. There has to be a position to put you in and there just aren't any. You'd need to be at least a nurse's aide for me to put you on the payroll to work in the infirmary."

"Who's taking care of the older ladies, Warden? Are they doing okay?"

The warden shrugged. "The infirmary staff is doing the best they can." Then she smiled at Evelyn. "They do miss you in there, Evelyn." She paused, frowning, chewing on her lip. "The only way I can use you, Evelyn, is as a volunteer. You can help out in the infirmary, just like you used to, but I can't pay you anything. You can have your meals in the mess hall, but you've got to be out of here after the evening meal. That's all I can do for you."

Evelyn grinned, showing her dentures. "That would be fine, ma'am. That would be just fine."

The warden stood. "You doing all right at the halfway house? You got money to get back and forth on the bus?"

Evelyn and Leena Mae had stood with the warden. "I'm doing fine there, Warden. And I've saved some money over the years. I can manage the bus fare."

The next day, when she finished her shift, Leena Mae waited until she saw Evelyn being let through the last exit gate then she followed her, stopped her outside. "Well, Evelyn, you're leaving a little late tonight." She looked Evelyn over. "You're looking better, even managed to sneak in a shower, I see."

Evelyn looked at Leena Mae then looked away. "Yes, I was feeling kind of sweaty. It's been a busy day. Lucille's beginning to get kind of hard to handle."

"When did you leave the halfway house, Evelyn?" Leena Mae

asked, peering at Evelyn's face in the gathering dusk. "And don't try to tell me you're still there. You've been showing up every morning before the bus even comes out this way."

Evelyn looked up at her. "They put me in with four other women, one of them with green hair and an earring in her nose. Another woman offered to get me drugs." She shook her head. "I've been used to better than that. I just couldn't stay there."

"So where *are* you staying?" Leena Mae smiled, put her hand on Evelyn's shoulder. "I just want to make sure you're all right, Evelyn. That's all."

Evelyn was silent for a moment then she turned, pointed toward a wooded area at the far end of the prison compound. "I'm staying down there," she said. "I got me a sleeping bag from a place called Goodwill. I got me an alarm clock so I'll always be on time. I even got me a little radio. I sleep outside, look up at the sky. It's nice back there." She looked worriedly up at Leena Mae. "You're not going to tell the warden, are you, ma'am? I'm happy now. About as happy as I've ever been, I guess."

Leena Mae shook her head. "Just let me know if you need anything. Okay? It's going to get wet and it's going to get cold."

Evelyn nodded. "I've got a little money and I've got Goodwill. I'll be all right." She looked up at Leena Mae in the near darkness. She smiled. "It just feels good to be close to home," she said.

About the author:

Paul Perry has been writing short fiction for thirty years with more than 150 stories published, most of them in literary magazines. He had a collection of 24 short stories entitled "Street People" published in October 2000 by Pocol Press of Cliftron, VA. Paul, in his late teens, spent almost two years living on the streets. He writes mostly about homeless people, hitchhikers, prostitutes, outsiders—those whom Paul refers to as "Dispossessed People."

CHARLES EDWARD CUNNINGHAM
©2000 by Ann G. Thomas

THEY TALKED ABOUT everyone, as if gossip were a required employee contribution to their meager compensation package— who was improving, who failing, who creating problems, who imparting wisdom. Some patients were more interesting than others but none, in the memory of any of the current staff, was generating more interest than the man in Room 21. He was gracious, cooperative, and quite good looking for someone his age.

May was the first among the staff to mention, "I hear him talking to someone but when I go in, there is no one there. He tells me he's talking to his friend, Cindy."

"Poor dear," someone responded. "Probably he's had another little stroke."

As his overheard conversations grew more frequent and the notations on his chart more numerous, the doctors began to show interest.

"Alzheimer's?" one said. "Mini-strokes?" said another. "Depression?" suggested a third, "or maybe paranoia". But no diagnosis proved true and the gossip began to dwindle. Many older patients talked to themselves. He was becoming just one patient among many until a strange thing happened. Someone reported they had heard a second voice, if only for a word or two, coming from his room. The next day someone else heard the voice and reported it was definitely that of a woman. After that, staff slowed outside his door to listen until the Director issued a memo:

Eavesdropping Won't Be Tolerated.

"It's not like he causes any trouble," May said. "If he wants to entertain..."

"It's a sight better than what some do to keep themselves amused," another added and everyone laughed.

Still, although many continued to hear what sounded like a woman's voice, no one ever saw him with anyone. "Maybe he's disguising his voice," someone said. The talk went on. Forbidden to eavesdrop, staff began to find reasons to visit, but even with this, they never saw a woman.

Then one night, May, tired from having worked a double shift, sent word around to hurry and finish evening duties. She had news. By ten-fifteen everyone was gathered at the brightly lit Nurses Station. Long halls stretched outward in three directions dotted on each side with the open doors of patients who lay sleeping or watching memories.

"Tell us, May."

"Well," she looked around, savoring her temporary importance, "I heard her. I was directly outside his door, closed mind you, and I could hear her voice as clear as I can hear you—not just a word but whole sentences."

"No! What was she saying? Who was it? What on earth did you do?" All eyes were glued on May. "Too much overtime," someone interjected.

"What did I do? Well, I opened the door and . . ." she paused, loving the suspense.

"What? What did you see? Who is she? I knew he had a woman in there, the old fox!"

"What I saw was him. No one else, just him, sitting there as calm as could be. There was no one else in the room."

"No way! What did he say? Did you ask him?"

"Well, of course. I said, 'Well, Mr. Cunningham. I heard a woman talking to you.' He just smiles that charming smile of his and says, 'Yes, Miss May. My friend Cindy was here. You just missed her.'

"Well, I didn't know what to say to that. I looked around—I mean, I couldn't very well look under his bed, but I did look everywhere else. No one! Not another living soul! So I says to him, 'and just exactly where did your friend Cindy go?'"

"And? What did he say to that?"

"Nothing. He just smiles at me. Not another word!"

"Write it up, May. You have to put this in his file for the psychiatrist."

"I suppose. It's just—well, I hate writing it. They might drug him."

"It was you heard the woman talking, May. Maybe they'll drug *you.*"

Everyone laughed, then continued their theories and speculation. Their words floated away to enter the open door of Room 21 and circle the sleeping man.

His name was Charles Edward Cunningham. If he heard the words, he gave no sign. By night he slept and by day he did whatever was required with dignity and pleasant charm.

He was here to rehabilitate from a stroke and, although he was gaining some strength and mobility, it was clear something wasn't right. When asked how he felt, his reply was always, "Better today, thank you." When asked if he felt discouraged or depressed, his reply was "No, quite the opposite." But when asked about the conversations, he would smile and say nothing, as if the question were more puzzling than any answer might be. So on this night, as the staff's words circled his bed, they failed to land, moving instead like dust mites around and around.

When he had first arrived, someone had written on his door the name Charlie but that was soon corrected. Even as a small child, his short cotton pants buttoned to their matching shirt, he was addressed as Charles Edward. He wore the name like skin.

Charles Cunningham had been his father's name. The name, a watch, a long-faded picture and his life were Charles Edward's legacy from this man he had never known. His father had died within hours of depositing his contribution to Charles Edward's life within his mother.

"Your father was a very successful man, Charles Edward, and he left me with the best part of himself," his mother had always said. "It was his final act upon this earth—to give me you. I do believe he knew somehow how much I needed him to leave me a fine little man in his place."

As a child, Charles Edward stood silent beneath these words. There seemed, to his young mind, nothing that needed to be said in reply; nor did his mother seem to encourage or even expect a response. It was her responsibility, she often said, to pass on family history. Charles Edward Cunningham's role was to listen and to find a place within himself where her words could settle. He was too young to recognize any difficulty with this arrangement.

"Edward," she told him, "was my daddy's name. Oh, Charles Edward, you would have just loved your granddaddy." She would look away, then sigh and bring her attention back to the small boy standing in front of her. "Two fine men, Charles Edward," she would say. "Two fine men who are part of you. You are the only man I have left now." And she would smile at him in what was meant to be an encouraging way.

Although it is difficult to know for certain, it appeared that Charles Edward did grow up to be like his mother's image of his male progenitors. On those occasions when it was appropriate to speak of another, Charles Edward was spoken of with high regard. Men saw him as responsible and fair—a man of character and integrity. He married for the first and only time when he was fifty, two years after his mother's death, and when his wife died five years later, there seemed to be a consensus among the men that if anyone could handle such a maiming, it was Charles Edward. They watched in silence as he moved through those days quietly, handling details or comforting others. While everyone offered condolences, no one tried to offer comfort, nor would Charles Edward have known how to take it in.

After the first year of obligatory distance to show respect for the dead, the women began circling. Charles Edward occasionally accepted invitations or issued those of his own but no relationship moved beyond an evening of theater or dinner. No woman was ever invited to cross the boundary into his home. Although many felt something deep within stir, urging them to reach out to Charles Edward, a silent something stopped them.

That was then. Now, eighteen years and one stroke later, Charles Edward Cunningham was residing in Room 21. The room he moved into contained the standard issue of furniture that was provided for residents who choose not to bring their own things—a single bed, dresser, bed table, chair and lamp. It stayed like that until a month ago with no pictures, no books, no personal belongings on the dresser—nothing except for the few clothes in the closet and a walker that stood waiting without comment for the times it was needed.

The daily florist delivery was the first change. Included with the many "Feel better Grandma" bouquets was a vase of roses addressed to him. No card was attached.

"I ordered them," he told curious staff and his fresh flowers began arriving regularly.

Two weeks after that initial delivery, a second bouquet arrived for the Nurses Station, again with no card although everyone knew. Then, there was another change although no one mentioned it at first.

"He asked me if I had children," someone said one day, and another responded, "I found myself telling him about my divorce and he said some things that were actually helpful."

Still, there was never any conversation from him about the woman whose name was Cindy.

The stroke that was responsible for his admission had been a shock. However, he had improved quickly in the hospital and the doctors were optimistic that a short stay in the nursing home for rehabilitation would have him back on his feet. The short stay, however, turned into three months, then six, and now eight and optimism turned into a vague type of waiting although neither he nor others spoke of this. Meanwhile, the conversations began.

It had been a Tuesday morning on the last day of Charles Edward Cunningham's second month in Room 21 when the knock came at the door. Charles Edward was resting in his chair, tired from the effort of dressing and shaving and walking the length of the hallway to the dining room for breakfast.

"Yes?"

"I'm Cindy. May I come in?"

"Please do." It was gracious, a response from years of politeness. He took a deep breath, wanting to be able to handle whatever this was to be about. She crossed the room toward him—small and blond with a floating style of walking. He noticed the way people walked these days. She brought to his mind a picture he had seen some seventy years ago of a fairy. He tried to remember the picture—a woodcut perhaps from some child's book of tales, but the title wouldn't come to his mind. She looked like a child herself, but he knew it was his own years that determined that perspective. She was probably somewhere in her late twenties, just a few years younger than a granddaughter would be if he had children. Her eyes were a clear blue and looked directly into his.

"You've been alone," she said.

Charles Edward sat silent. There seemed, to his mind, nothing to say in reply nor did Cindy seem to expect a response. She sat on the edge of the bed facing his chair and began to talk in a soft and floating voice while he listened with only an occasional comment. At the end of an hour she left. When he tried to remember afterward, no words came to him. All he had left from the visit was a feeling of warmth. It made him angry.

By the second visit he realized she was not part of the staff. He thought to ask her who had sent her but, once she began talking, it slipped his mind. After a few visits it seemed unimportant and when those from the staff began asking him questions, he didn't respond. He was not a man to speak of others, even during his more talkative days, and speaking of her now seemed strangely wrong as if he were being asked to betray a confidence.

Cindy came each day. He grew to look forward to, and finally to depend on, her visits. At the same time, his days were growing fuller, although he didn't know why since he had little to do. There was the physical therapy of course, although they had ceased to make progress and were reaching a dead end, but even that was beginning to seem acceptable.

The pattern was the same each day—meals, doctors, and therapy. Somehow Cindy's visits never conflicted and yet she never missed a day. With her arrival, he would feel oxygen fill his lungs. She would reach out and touch his hand, brushing her lips across his cheek and he could feel her energy circling first above and then around until some type of merging seemed to occur. She had become his breath and his light. He understood something he had never understood before, although he would not have been able to put into words exactly what that was.

It was only a few days after May had asked him about Cindy that the worst of all imaginings happened. He woke with a strange feeling, attributing it to fatigue since he had stayed up later than usual the night before. He was anxious to see Cindy since the visits energized him, but the morning passed, then afternoon tea and finally the supper hour and Cindy did not come. "She is only late," he reasoned to himself, although he knew.

He was unable to eat lunch, staying in his room so as not to miss her, although he knew she never came at mealtime. Tea came and went without his presence and supper held no interest. By seven that evening, Charles Edward Cunningham was beside himself. He changed into his pajamas and went to bed. The charge nurse took his temperature and blood pressure, duly noting that Mr. C. E. Cunningham, Room 21, was lethargic and had declined lunch, tea and dinner although his vital signs exhibited no change from normal.

Charles Edward was unable to sleep. He lay there, visualizing Cindy and wondering what had kept her from him. She had not missed a day since—how long had it been? Three or four months at least, maybe longer. He felt twinges of a deep anger pulsing in rhythm within the abyss of longing. The pain wracking his body was worse than the stroke had been. He bore the pain with difficulty. Much of the silent, indomitable strength of his forefathers had become eroded during these past few months. He drew his legs upward toward his belly, curling around the pain while rocking himself back and forth. He wanted her with a rawness he had never felt before. His voice was silent but his being cried for her. Sleep would not come.

At a little after midnight he heard a movement. He looked toward the door, expecting a night nurse and saw instead Cindy. She moved toward the bed. As he sat up she gathered him into her arms. Tears began to flow from his eyes down the gullies of his lined face.

"I thought," he began. "I'm sorry." He tried to stop the tears, fearing she would think less of him.

"Hush," she said. "I'm here now. Cry." She wrapped him tightly in her arms while he sobbed tears that had perhaps been stored since that day when, just beginning to float within his own mother's womb, he knew of his father's death. He cried for the boy who never lived in his boy body. He cried for the mother who wanted a man instead of a child. He cried for the wife he loved but was always afraid to touch. He cried until he could cry no more, while Cindy held him to her breast. And then, as she opened her blouse, he did what he had never dared to do during all the years of his marriage, or even what he had never been invited to do as an infant. He took the nipple she offered into his mouth and allowed himself to drink from the depth of this woman. He sucked while she held him and as he did, her breasts grew large and larger and her milk began to flow. He drank while she held him and soon she began to hum, rocking him gently back and forth.

He did not know when he fell asleep. When he awoke she was gone. Only her milk remained, deep within his being. Only her touch remained, caressing his skin.

Somehow, he knew she would not be back, but it no longer mattered, for he knew he would not stay. Something very important had changed. He could not tell if the change was within or without, but he knew it was there, circling and circling. Down his long hallway the nightly words began to float from those at the Nurse's Station.

"Who? Is there a no-code?" The words faded, drowned out by the soft, circling hum of a woman's voice.

"Stay with me, Mr. Cunningham!" a loud voice said, but he closed his ears to the sound. Only the humming mattered and he felt himself joining the sound, circling further and further away from Room 21.

Everyone who was anyone came to the funeral—the mayor, the governor, business tycoons from his former life. Only Charles Edward Cunningham failed to attend.

About the Author:

Ann G. Thomas: teacher, writer and psychotherapist. In private practice in California as a psychotherapist since 1978 with specialties in child development and geriatrics. Writes both fiction and non-fiction including numerous magazine articles on aging. Her book, "The Women We Become" (Prima, 1997) was recently reprinted in paperback and translated into three languages for overseas sale.

CELEBRATION OF LOVE
©1999 by Elaine Elizabeth Papp

"I NEED TO speak with someone immediately!" Sherry screamed into the phone. She had never been a short-tempered person, but after being placed on hold, passed from one person to another, and finally transferred to an answering machine, she'd lost it.

After all, her wedding was in three days and the bridesmaids' dresses had been delivered in purple, not the soft lavender she'd ordered, mind you, or even a gentle mauve. No! a bright glaring purple. Thinking back to the tiny bunches of Baby's Breath she'd carefully chosen for the girls to wear in their hair, she could almost cry. Who would even notice them now? Of course, she was being overly dramatic, but her entire life had been spent planning things right down to the smallest detail. And, even though her friends had tried to warn her that weddings usually had last minute problems, she had quietly listened while smiling and smugly thinking, "Not my wedding, I'm too well prepared."

She immediately called Tom to tell him about the catastrophe and he'd responded exactly the way she had expected, "Don't worry, Sweetie, everything will be wonderful anyway."

"How like him," she groaned. Neither of them were rattled by problems: she, because she never left anything to chance and he, because nothing seemed to bother him.

Last week, while having a few last-minute wedding jitters, she had questioned why she was marrying someone so totally different from herself and knew immediately that the real question was, "Why was *he* marrying *her*?" He was so good looking it scared her. He had that casual, wind-blown, perpetually tan look that most women loved and a cheeky little smile that seldom left his face. Friendly and charming to everyone, he was completely unaware of the magnetism and charm that emanated from within and never noticed the admiring glances thrown his way. Generally, the center of attraction at gatherings, people naturally gravitated to his looks, his charm, and his easy wit.

If Sherry's friends were asked to list her attributes, they'd probably say, "She's such a nice person, so sweet and so very competent. Why, give her any task and she'll complete it properly and on time."

"What a testimonial," Sherry thought. All of her friends had loved Tom from the start and often teased that she'd better hold on tight. She knew they were kidding, but couldn't help wondering if what they were really saying was, "What in the world does he see in her?"

All right, so she knew that she wasn't totally unattractive, just appealing in a controlled sort of way. Her hair was cut just short enough to ensure that it stayed in place and her carefully applied make-up looked precisely the same way every day. Having always been a conservative dresser, Sherry selected her clothing carefully, making sure that each blouse, pair of pants or sweater had its own match. Better than anyone, she knew that there wasn't a spontaneous bone in her whole body.

Okay, so she knew why she'd chosen Tom, why had he chosen her? There were prettier women, more outgoing women, and certainly more exciting women and yet, in her heart, she knew that his feelings were genuine. She saw that every time he looked into her eyes or said her name all breathy and with a catch in his throat. How could she inspire the passion he seemed to feel?

This was why the details of the wedding were so important to Sherry. She wanted the wedding to be perfect for Tom, not because he demanded perfection, but rather as her gift to him. Since he had refused to wait longer, they had planned their entire wedding in less than three months. Together, they'd found an adorable church on a hill and the wedding was set to take place at 2:00 p.m. this Saturday. Originally, Tom had suggested an outdoor wedding, but Sherry had reminded him that a rainy day might ruin the reception. Next, he had casually mentioned that a camping trip to the Catskills might make a wonderful location for a honeymoon and, laughing, Sherry had convinced him to fly to Bermuda.

Suddenly, her phone rang and, grabbing it quickly, she answered, "Good morning, Sherry McKenzie speaking. How may I help you?"

"Sherry, good afternoon, it's Kelly from Bridal Expressions returning your call. I'm sorry to hear that there's a slight problem with the shade of purple you chose for the gowns."

"Slight?" Sherry's face flooded with color as a sense of foreboding swept over her. It was suddenly crystal clear that, despite all her planning, things were not going to go according to plan. "I wouldn't call it slight; the color is all wrong—"

Not giving Sherry time to continue, Kelly interrupted. "Well, as you know, everything was *rushed*. You didn't exactly give us much time to place the order and, of course, everyone knows that color swatches are never perfect. Oh well, can I assume that you didn't give us the correct date for the wedding? I am right, aren't I? No one ever does. So, hopefully, there will be plenty of time to exchange the dresses. When *is* the actual wedding date, Dear?"

Sherry's head began to pound as she whispered, "What do you mean I didn't give you the correct wedding date? Of course, I did. Is there some kind of wedding etiquette that says I shouldn't?"

"Well," Kelly responded, "It's practically an unwritten law. Everyone knows that you never give the correct date so that when problems arise, there's time to fix them."

In spite of her best efforts, Sherry voice quavered as she replied, "Well, I didn't know so what can we do now?"

"Well..." Kelly hesitated to give the impression that she'd just come up with a clever idea. "How about if I give you a fifteen percent discount on the dresses?"

"No, that's not acceptable!" Sherry's voice grew stronger as indignation set in.

"All right, Sherry, make it twenty percent, but that's my final offer. It is, after all, only a small problem, not exactly the end of the world, you know."

In spite of her frustration, Sherry couldn't help noticing that the more annoyed Kelly became the more her upper class Boston accent seemed to vanish.

Without stopping to take a breath, Kelly continued, "Bye, bye, Sherry. Best wishes on your wedding day. We'll all be thinking about you. Please don't feel that you have to thank me for the discount. Bridal Expressions does whatever they can for their brides." And with that sentiment, Kelly quickly disconnected the call, ensuring that Sherry had no time to respond.

Placing her hands on her throbbing head, Sherry moaned, "How am I going to tell Tom that I can't fix the dresses?" She honestly knew that he wouldn't be mad and would probably just laugh it off, but would that mean that he just didn't care?

Deep in thought, Sherry jumped as her phone rang again, "Hello, Sherry McKenzie speaking, how may I help you?"

"Sherry...hello, it's Henré from Starlight Catering. How are you doing, Dear? Listen, a problem has come up regarding your reception. I know you're not going to believe this, but the condenser on our air conditioning unit went out just this morning and I've spent what feels like an eternity on the phone talking to the repairman. He insists that there is no possible way that the new unit can be installed in time for your reception. You just wouldn't believe the morning I've had...but I guess you're not interested in my problems."

Henré chuckled before rattling on, "I—well, we're going to have to come up with some sort of solution for your reception. I know this seems unbelievable, but I can assure you that nothing like this has ever happened to us before. I know you'll understand that this isn't our fault. So, what do you think, Love? Do you have any suggestions?"

Too stunned to speak, Sherry's mouth hung open as she tried to form the words to answer him.

To Henré, however, her silence came across as disapproval and, sounding annoyed, he continued, "Well...look...if you'd rather deal with another caterer, I'll understand."

This blew Sherry's mind as she sputtered and choked, "What do you mean 'deal with another caterer'? The wedding is in less than three days. What am I supposed to do, start over?"

"Well, Dearie...think about the possibility of splitting the rental of a hall with us and we'll be happy to bring everything there. Nothing overly expensive, I hope, and of course, you won't have our view of the rose garden, but we'll do our best. You must understand that this was totally unexpected. Listen, let me give you a call later tonight after we've both had time to think of a solution."

Like Kelly, Henré hung up quickly before Sherry had time to respond. Groaning, she thought back to the first time they'd spoken with Kelly and Henré. She'd been impressed with both their polish and their expertise, but Tom had immediately complained that they were both stuffed shirts and had said laughingly, "Oh please Sherry, Henré. You know his name is probably Henry and as far as Kelly is concerned, she's never been a mile north of Brooklyn."

At the time, she'd just shaken her head and muttered, "Men," but now, Kelly and Henré were acting as if everything was her fault.

An unusual sense of panic began flooding her mind as the room began to spin and the walls closed in around her. Jumping from her desk, she ran from her office and headed toward the ladies room. The closer she got to the door, the faster she ran and the harder the tears streamed down her face. It was while rounding the last corner at a dead run that Sherry glanced back and found the entire office staff staring at her and whispering. The last face she saw through her veil of tears was that of her best friend Kera.

Charging into the ladies room, she collapsed on a chair near the door before seeing Sonja, the office manager, standing by the sink. Sonja immediately asked if she could help, but Sherry, unable to answer, rocked back and forth, sobbing as if her heart would break.

The door slammed against the wall and Tom burst into the room. His office was in the next building and, obviously, Kera must have called him immediately. Without a word to either woman, he picked Sherry up in his arms and, lowering her head to his shoulder, sat on the chair. A wonderful, warm feeling flooded her entire being. Not since her mother's death had the strong, independent and slightly self-righteous woman felt the need to have someone to lean on. She had loved Tom before, but now for the first time, she realized that Tom's carefree attitude was for the rest of the world. For her and her alone, he'd always show a different, softer side where his protection, his caring and, most of all, his love would continue to surround her.

Suddenly, Sherry realized that neither the color of the bridesmaids' dresses nor the elegant reception in the beautiful hall really mattered. She finally understood that their wedding was a celebration of their love and a reaffirmation of their commitment to each other. Looking deep into Tom's eyes, she saw that he was quietly waiting for her to explain how he could help.

As suddenly as they began, her tears dried and her face lit up with love as she blurted out, "Oh, Tom, you were right all along. An outdoor reception at the church on the hill would be perfect. Why, the flowers surrounding the church are in full bloom and couldn't be more beautiful. Let's move the time for the wedding back and take our vows under the stars. Afterwards, we can dance the night away in each other's arms."

Sherry smiled shyly into his loving eyes, "And, maybe, just maybe, you were right about the honeymoon, too."

Tom stood up and laughingly swung her around as he whispered into her ear, "Oh what an impulsive woman I'm marrying."

About the author:

Married for over thirty years to her first love Richard, Elaine enjoys writing about a romantic innocence rarely found in today's fast-paced world. Her two grown sons and their wives have unknowingly been the source for many a short story while she is counting on the antics of Jonathan, her first grandchild, to inspire many more. Having lived for the past five years in Washington Crossing, Pennsylvania, Elaine and her husband enjoy bicycling at the Washington Crossing Historic Park and along the Delaware-Raritan Canal. "Celebration of Love" is her first publication.

AUTUMN
©2000 by Janice Lynn Mather

A FRIGID HOSPITAL space.

Desiree hates the place, room robbed daily of its protective dust, tiles scrubbed of grubbiness, but scarred from harsh wheels of beds and obese, movable machines raked screechingly, cruelly over the floor. Mattress soft as a boney, flat-chested woman is for a small, cold child to cuddle, slips vindictively off wire-intertwined bedframe. Blood stained sheets, bleached clinically clean, yet scarred filthy forever psychologically, smudged hints of red from earlier chapters of her story, sheets that won't stay tucked in give no cosiness in cold, central air-controlled building.

And there is no bedspread here to keep her warm.

A skinny woman wearing comically lightened hair that refuses to match her sun-weathered, leathered flesh stands at the foot of the bed. She claims to be a dietitian as she casually twines her maimed mane around fingers tipped with cherry-coloured painted nails. Desiree lies back, lowers disinterested eyes, understands why men of medicine hang ten or so crooked certificates on bare walls between charts of average weight-to-height ratios; it gives credibility, some cause to nod in blind agreement with the diagnosis of a ten-minutes-hence stranger. But this woman offers no proof that she brings truth as she spews would-be dietary facts at her, questioning her as to

"How many grams of fat do you eat daily? Do you record your fat intake? You should drink two percent milk (skim will keep you skinny), are you a vegetarian? That would cause weight loss too. I encourage low fat rather than no fat diets now, we used to discourage use of fat but we now know we need fat, now we know we get fat, good fat, from good sources: nuts, rich milks, eggs, cheese and—"

Please!

Desiree tunes out words, how can she hear the words of a woman thirty years older than she is on a topic like this, topic she bases her life, her happiness around?

"Any questions?" the brittle-haired woman barks, almost demanding comment, query.

Yes,

Desi wants to ask, *Have you*
ever fit into a
size two or
smaller?
You look like you
wear a three,
you're not like me, weren't
teased endlessly
all through school, called
fat ass pig, big bitch, two-ton horse shit.
How can I
trust the advice of
some waif who wears
small jeans
effortlessly, it's
in your genes, you were born
small born
small born
thin born
to fit into
the thin trends of
the thin world we live in we
are drilled to be thin subtly, so

subliminally we
don't even notice till we
notice we're always
trying to
waste to
weight that less than ten percent of women
are fated to be
naturally.

"So, if you can increase your intake of high calorie carbohydrates we can get you to gain some weight, why don't I leave this diet sheet for you to follow, you need to gain some more weight."

more weight more
weight more
weighty matters weigh heavy on Desiree's mind, she likes herself fine as she finally is now, treasures how her boyfriend's hands meet around her waist, so small is it now, finds sleekness to her face quite enticing, hated when she used to be called

fat girl, fat face, fat chance anyone will like you, you don't look like flat bellied, big busted girls in glossy magazines who smile when you turn to their page, smile if you turn away, turn back again, still smiling, (is it that neat-nipped midsection that makes them happy?), close book, open again, see, she smiles still, permanently happy let me smile permanently too.

"You're clinically underweight," the slender dietitian is saying "You should fit somewhere between here and here," pointing at meaningless numbers on bland charts, the woman barks, bleats, makes incomprehensible animal noises Desi cannot hear: 120; 117; 111; 108; it means nothing to her. All she knows is, it hurts, it aches, it hates, the big thing in her skinny body that cries UGLY PIG when she sees happy girls wearing clothes smaller than her, how is it that they stay tiny, constantly consuming burgers dripping 14-g-of-f-a-t-per-t-b-s-p mayonnaise, and ketchup, stretchy-stringed full-fat cheese, and oil-soaked French fries?

How is it that the sight of a full plate of food before her eyes intended for her makes her feel physically sick?

The sheer insult, insinuating that she could eat a

whole potato, entire barbecued chicken quarter, cob of corn, and carrots!

The people in the kitchen here must think she is a glutton.

"...try for five pounds by end of November, okay? Be a good girl?" The born-skinny bitch smiles faux-camaraderie at Desiree who watches her leave with envy, will she, Desiree, ever be

petite enough, petite

enough? Enough for who, for

what?

Why? Desiree begins to cry, effort of exertion of agony of she who believes she will always be chubby, leaves her weary, so pitiful. She lifts an arm thinner than it was when she was six, she is sick is

sick is

sickened by the fallaway of her breasts, of where her breasts would be if she was bigger, still she is bigger than some women are made, she is not maddened anymore by her body, only saddened, so worn, so worn, so

she reaches for the flip switch blade from beneath the mattress, where she hides it from nurses who change permanently bloodied sheets on harsh, wire-intertwined bedframe, reaches, pulls it out, flips it open, eyes focus on wrist (her veins are so easy to see these days, uninterrupted underneath the skin by bothersome, unwanted flesh). She starts to raise her hand, her wrist, her life is mutated into an ugly cycle of tears, fainting, sickening, admissions to doctors' visits, chidings by strangers to eat to eat to be

the opposite of what her mind is trained to want to be. Lowers knife towards her wrist, scratches with it, firmer, barely breaks skin she is so thin yet so weak, so

fat, she

feels the knife slip out of reach, it makes a cold, harsh tinkle-noise on the tiled hard floor, she reaches for it, wants to try again to end, reaches further, (life is out of reach,) she slips she falls she

falls she
falls, a noise of nothing more than bones and skin descending,
makes a sound little louder than that of dry leaves falling,
falling.
She is too weak to rise again.

About the author:

Janice Lynn Mather was born in Nassau, Bahamas on December 29, 1981. Her love of writing dates back almost that far, though her skill is still in its developing stages. Her career goal is to prove that creative writing is a viable career for Bahamian women. She is currently pursuing further studies in the art of writing. "Autumn" is her first published work.

THE WITNESS
©2001 by Christopher T. Bowne

A BUSINESSMAN—*a self-made man*, his obituary reads—had of late found it necessary to jog around and through the community park after work several days a week under doctor's orders. His business, though suddenly successful beyond anyone's expectations and appearing to run under its own volition, was taking a toll on his health. The doctors advised exercise, among other things (caffeine reduction, fish pills, etc.), if he hoped to avoid a heart attack. "We have heart disease on all sides," his sister declared, "all the way up both family trees."

One Thursday in early Spring, the businessman noted his schedule was clear for the rest of the day, took off early—calling his sister before he left—and was soon jogging the park, said his sister, steering clear, as he always did, of the park botanical gardens, which exacerbated his allergies. This detour unavoidably pressed him into some of the less popular areas of the park. "If it hadn't been for his allergies, he'd be with us today," his sister lamented after the funeral.

He was jogging through these, some would say, gloomier regions ("malignant", his sister called them) when a man sitting at a park bench adjacent to his path "must have said something," said the only witness, himself sitting off in the background unobserved against a tree, "taking it all in," he said. The jogger-businessman passed the man on the bench, the bench-sitter—"sitting on the top part of the bench, the backrest, with his feet on the seat and constantly wiping his nose," observed the witness—but not before saying "Ha!" loudly. "Bellowed it, really—just as my father would," the witness offered. "My father would bellow 'Ha!' without fail every time he beat me at chess, to humiliate me and exalt himself. He could not bring himself to beat me physically, though I know he wanted to. He was not the physical type. He, in fact, was always saying how he hated the physical types, 'the sporty types are the worst,' he'd always say," said the witness. "No, he was all about the brain—so he beat me at chess, which he probably told himself was more complete in its effect. I *always* agreed to these games, these endurance tests, in hopes of beating him, was tantalized by this thought, and would immediately and perversely accept any game he hung under my nose, knowing all too well I would not win, could not in fact win, actually fearing that I might (what would happen?), yet unable to stop myself—going in like a dog. I would go into these games, basically, a dog to a whipping. In my father's hands," said the witness, "chess became a weapon, and the game, a beating, but only because of the capper: his signature 'Ha!' that punctuated the game; the final move inevitably in his favor. The second he said 'Ha!' the game of chess as we know it, and specifically, the history of the game played up to that moment, was destroyed; erected in its place was this massive *world-view* weapon hacking away immediately and ruthlessly at retrospect— this 'Ha!' chess weapon. This 'Ha!' chess weapon and its constituent parts defined our relationship," said the witness. "For a second, I thought it was my father all over again, even as I was watching this jogger bellow 'Ha!' right before my eyes. For a second, I was no longer in the park."

According to the witness, this was all that the jogger-businessman said, "said without stopping, *without even looking*," the witness asserted. "He didn't need to look, he'd said it all." What happened next was: the bench-sitter got up off the bench, looked at the ground a little, picked up a stone and immediately threw it, "half-heartedly," said the witness, bringing down the jogger-businessman at about forty yards "—like a dog."

"It all happened quickly, but in a half-hearted manner," said the witness. The bench-sitter, standing for a pause, then ran off. "This bench-sitter from the very beginning struck me as indecisive," said the witness. "Everything he did spoke hesitancy. Something I noticed immediately was his clothing; his clothing seemed all wrong: confused and haggled over, as if the most exhausted effort had been put into dressing himself that morning and by looking at him, at the various stress folds and color splotches, one could read the pain and fatigue and general torridness of this endeavor. I sat there observing him sit at the bench, perched on the top part ('perched' better describes it) for nearly two hours and in the course of these two hours of close and continual observation, I noted over and over that he was always on the verge of getting up—was, in fact, always getting up and always sitting down simultaneously. Getting up and sitting down, sitting down and getting up again, over and over, such that he seemed nearly to hover in mid-air ('hover' best describes it!). He was constantly wiping his nose during this ritualized movement, this, in the end, *dance of indecisiveness*—no doubt a common affliction these days," agreed the witness. "This nose wiping (its phrasing and pacing) as opposed to his other characteristics (perching, hovering, clothing), was always pulled off with the utmost conviction, with not the least bit of hesitation, and most likely had its source in torment from the winds that sometimes carry a touch of the botanical gardens in them. This nose wiping, which never let up, and its associated pattern of occurrence proved his only decisive feature."

The witness read off the daily paper: the jogger-businessman had suffered lacerations to the knees and face, and a fractured skull. For a time, he seemed to be getting better (the witness read this phrase with an incredulous tone), but died suddenly three weeks later in his hospital bed with his entire family gathered round and his mother arriving just hours before it happened, sitting silently through the whole ordeal, and leaving silently afterwards without speaking to anyone, leaving, as it were, vacant in eye. The doctor, a family friend, put into his report as cause of death: "'An undiagnosed blood clot in the left frontal lobe,'" read the witness. As a man in full bloom and bloviating (the witness pointed at the photo adjacent the article), the doctor spoke plainly during a public address: "'He will be in all our hearts, but he was taken down in his prime, his family's life shattered, all by a brainless, spineless hooligan, a sorely misguided youth without a conscience. The signs were there—still are. We must not be complacent. Let us see this as a lesson, good people!'"

The witness continued reading: the bench-sitter was never found; the police were at a loss; the papers went on about the history of that unique spot in the park, about all the signs, all that could have been done. "'The people and their *drug-haven*,'" the witness noted aloud. "Look here," pointed the witness, "the phrase *famous and beloved chess tables* and *botanical garden* together in one sentence, not far from the drug-haven—here they're placing the crime, no doubt," said the witness, "and standing up to anonymity." The witness read the sentence out loud: "'The crime occurred in an area coined by some residents as a drug haven, not all together distant from the community's famous and beloved chess tables, as well as the century-old botanical garden.'"

"The context of the death," said the witness, "not the death itself is the wellspring of this article. There is no longer any death, only *death-in-context*; a man dies and we're confronted with the *drug-havens* and *botanical gardens*—say, somewhere an old widow hears mention of *gondolas* or is confronted with the word *mudflats*; the poor woman is thrown into convulsions, and death's pall hangs for days or weeks, crushing her—so you see, this or that man is at once bound to these words, ensnared, in his death, in these words—words he'd immediately walk (or jog!) away from in life, but now, in death, is helpless against, as a fly in a web." The witness added that, incidentally, as a teenager he'd spent an entire summer among the chess tables polishing his game, subsisting entirely on blueberries and coffee, and mindfully avoiding the botanical gardens to which he was extremely allergic.

"Because my father used chess as a weapon against me," said the witness, "I was forced, on my own, to study chess carefully. I allowed myself no choice on the matter while, at the same time, knowing I really had no choice, or so I fancied to think. I entered the so-called chess world—everything within the constellation of chess, with special attention given to the game itself—played tournaments, won, climbed the ranks in this world, first in my head then in reality; each opponent placed in front of me in the flesh was superfluous, yet crucial and was defeated thus: superfluously and crucially, physically-mentally, mentally-physically. I climbed right up this world in a mental-physical manner, won the North American Grandmaster title. When I claimed this prize, against my father of course, which, when held up on its own merits, was a total joke (mentally and physically!) I was immediately aware that my father, from then on, was finished absolutely, washed up; this was obviously so, embarrassingly so— especially since he had been in the grave for over a year. Such absurd lengths I went! I thought at my supposed moment of triumph, what have I done? My father—putrefying in the grave, nothing but worms! I dropped it all instantly. The chess world was laid over him, itself laid over by deliberate memory loss; the memory of the chess world, and the special attention necessarily given to the game itself, was shrugged off, killed off, buried, et cetera . . .now underground. The chess world had become, for all practical purposes, a corpse. Though it was apparently not apparent to the others, I killed off the entire chess world mentally the instant they called my name to the podium to accept the prize," said the witness, "and the entire act of receiving this prize became a shameful exercise (I had to be helped from my seat), consisting of nothing more than walking up a corpse, receiving this corpse to its own grotesque applause, stammering a prepared speech to the corpse, and leaving the corpse behind forever."

"Now I look around and see the sneezing, see the basic underlying suffering, and I say," said the witness, "these people, such and such persons, who in all respects should never be within miles of each other, who share common violent reactions to particular aspects of the world, particular menaces of the world—menaces that inspire violent and or allergic blindly reactive outbursts (and so can justly be called menaces)—are, in the end, being repelled into various toxic configurations with each other by these *enmity-propagating* menaces, which are, of course, everywhere," said the witness. "I immediately understand this, this general tendency in humans and such—this relationship between the individuals and their allotted menaces, their tendencies towards these menaces; each other, and their tendencies towards each other; each other with respect to each menace and so forth—this tendency towards *total combustion of everything*. Of course, the incident with the jogger-businessman and all of it was but one example of this. Of course, too, I look at myself, *must* look at myself, as someone no less susceptible to these tendencies. I look at myself and say," said the witness "I am no less susceptible."

A renaissance of sorts came to that region of sidewalk, turf, and trees, prompted by a month long "Take Back the Park" campaign. The bench was removed. There was increased foot traffic of several varieties. The witness retired to silence among the low rises struck with trees, stationing himself amidst shade and new insects, and half-hidden from eyes warily attuned to their surroundings.

About the author:

Christopher was born in 1973 in Newport Beach, CA. In his youth he spent a lot of time drawing, ignoring his studies, and obsessing over movies, girls, music, and skateboards. He holds a degree in Mathematics from UC Berkley. He began writing diligently last year after a ten-year hiatus. He now works in San Francisco and resides in Oakland.

www.ingramcontent.com/pod-product-compliance
Lightning Source LLC
Chambersburg PA
CBHW061206170626
46809CB00003B/1260